When blizzards disrupt Sister Peta Blair's travel plans, she's content to spend Christmas working on her children's ward—until she discovers that her troublesome new tenant, globetrotting surgeon Ashley Reeves, is also going to be there!

CANDLES FOR THE SURGEON

BY
HELEN UPSHALL

MILLS & BOON LIMITED
15–16 BROOK'S MEWS
LONDON W1A 1DR

First published in Great Britain
by Mills & Boon Limited

© Helen Upshall 1984

Australian copyright 1984
Philippine copyright 1984
This edition 1984

ISBN 0 263 74886 3

Set in 11 on 12 pt Linotron Times
03–1284–47,000

Photoset by Rowland Phototypesetting Ltd
Bury St Edmunds, Suffolk
Made and printed in Great Britain by
Richard Clay (The Chaucer Press) Ltd
Bungay, Suffolk

CHAPTER ONE

PETA stirred beneath her warm sheets. She lifted her face and twitched her nose. Surely the heating must have come on by now? Then she remembered that it was already on with the thermostat lowered. She'd switched on the override button last night when the weatherman warned of temperatures dropping below zero and forecast snow gradually expected to cover the country as the day progressed. She glanced at her bedside clock and was surprised to see that it was barely six-thirty.

She hated December mornings, but this one seemed different with an eery sort of light reflected behind the curtains. Today she was travelling to Sussex. From today she had no more hospital duties to consider until after Christmas. She covered her head with the sheet, wondering what madness had come over her to accept Ivor's invitation to spend the festive season with him and his family. She should have stuck out, been allowed to please herself, but, well, he was her brother, and he was doing his best to make up for everything.

She turned over and stretched. Tomorrow morning she'd have her twin nephews scrambling all over her, she supposed, and the new baby would frequently be dumped on her lap to be fed. It wasn't going to be much change from some of the things she did at Gida hospital situated on the outskirts of Exeter and named after a local eleventh century countess. How was Baby Alexander she wondered, and Baby Llewellyn? In her mind she went through the names on all the cots in the babies' ward, and with a grin she thought of the two or three little horrors in the boys' ward. Blah, Blah, Blah, they called her instead of Sister Blair, but she didn't mind. Oh dear, how she wished—but it was no use, she was going to Ivor's for Christmas and that was that.

It was horribly quiet, she decided after a few minutes. Usually by this time old Mrs Hubbard was at the door yelling for her nocturnal cat and Mr Amory was getting his car out of the garage opposite, singing or talking to himself. But it was Sunday and any sensible body would be doing exactly as Peta was doing, putting off getting up. It was no use, she'd have to make a move. She had packed in a disinterested kind of way last evening, but now she must discipline her mind to look forward to watching Peter and Paul delving into their stockings on Christmas morning, and she hoped they'd like the toys she'd bought.

They wouldn't, she knew. They were spoilt brats who had everything and expected each present to be bigger and better than the previous one. A sadness crept over her as she remembered her mother's arthritic fingers struggling to complete bobble caps and scarves last year, and all the boys did was toss them aside and look in the wrapping to see if they had missed anything. Greedy little devils, she thought angrily.

Mum was gone now. She'd found the winter ills too much to cope with, and with Dad going suddenly after a stroke less than two years ago it had been a rather bleak, miserable period. She was alone; no, Ivor and Ros, Peter, Paul and the babe were her family.

Peta sat up and stared into space. If only Ivor could understand that she needed to be kept busy, especially at this time of year. The poorly children of her ward wouldn't scorn their presents, and she had so wanted to be part of their Christmas morning.

She thought again of Ivor – Ivor the Terrible, as he'd been known in bygone days. He was five years older than Peta and she had always looked up to her big brother. He was tall and lean with dark hair and latterly a neatly clipped moustache which she laughingly thought of as his executive's brand. In colouring he was quite unlike Peta who was fair-haired, delicately pale-skinned, with sparkling cornflower blue eyes in contrast to Ivor's, which were a sombre brown.

Who'd have thought that he'd grow up to be so capable, so incredibly handsome – and so bossy! After repeated invitations to Peta to go to Sussex to live, he'd come lording it to Devon and had stood in the dining-room of the home her parents had created with such love.

'It's too big for just you, Pet. Now do be sensible, you simply can't afford the upkeep and I've got the boys, and—well—there's a new baby on the way, so—' He hadn't given her time to congratulate them before rushing on to say, 'Ros and I have decided that it would be best, if you're sure you won't come to Sussex, to make the house into self-contained flats and you can live in the top one. We'll let off the ground floor and you can bank the money it brings in, until you decide it's right to sell.'

'I *can't* sell yet!' she'd shrieked at her brother emotionally.

She buried her face in her hands. She didn't think she would ever be able to make a home anywhere but in this happy crescent. He'd been right, of course. Although she earned good money, a house this size was too expensive for her to keep up.

Ivor and Ros had tried a crafty move too, suggesting that the rent—when they eventually found a tenant—would be best paid to her. Then she could just pass half of it over to them. She'd be on hand to see to repairs and things, and didn't he pay enough income tax as it was in his posh job.

Peta had exploded. She was no fool. Didn't she pay tax the same as he? And unearned income on top of her modest salary would be a bigger sacrifice than for him with all his expense benefits and relief for a wife and two, no three, children. Brother Ivor hadn't reckoned with her business acumen, but she'd lived at home all her life except for early training days in a London hospital and she had learnt a great deal about practical matters from her parents, especially her accountant father.

Now the conversion had been completed and the flat was let, or supposed to have been, though Peta had heard no movements from downstairs in spite of the agent telephoning to say that the tenant expected to move in before Christmas.

With a sudden burst of energy she got out of bed. Perhaps Ivor was right. She'd grin and bear it in Sussex. It really didn't seem right to think of someone else being in the house over this first Christmas without Mum.

Peta yawned and stretched her slim, lithe body. The flat was pleasantly warm but she went through to the kitchen and turned up the thermostat control. She just hoped the water and everything would be all right in her absence. She filled the kettle and switched it on, then drew back the curtains. She couldn't believe her eyes. Snow was falling like great tufts of cotton wool, so thick she couldn't see to the other side of the road. Her wide-eyed gaze swept down to the ground. It must be inches thick!

Her brain was quick to grasp the situation. She'd just never make Sussex now!

She tried to keep calm. After telephoning the motoring services and listening to the radio she lifted her eyes heavenward and thanked God for His intervention. She needed several minutes to compose herself. She couldn't ring Ivor with jubilation in her voice! But in the event she didn't need to worry as, despite endless tries, she couldn't even get through. Main lines were down and a blizzard was on its way, even worse than the chaos already disrupting essential services. All of Great Britain was covered by a blanket of snow.

After the relief came a feeling of guilt. Ivor would feel he was letting her down, just as she inwardly experienced a pang of remorse. But neither of them could have foreseen this kind of weather. Suddenly she panicked. Was there a chance that the weather could change dramatically and the snow might disappear in the next few days so that she would still be expected to make a last minute journey?

Stop it, she reproached sharply. In the words of

her beloved Mum, whatever will be, will be, and it will be for the best.

Peta sighed. They'd been a close family until Ivor had married Ros and the family had started arriving. Ros was all right, even if she was the above average, intelligent type. Peta suspected, though, that her mind was usually somewhere other than on practical matters, so that the boys were wild and undisciplined.

Peta loved them and in all honesty had looked forward to seeing them again, but in a strange way the children in her care in Angelique ward needed her more than Peter, Paul and Bunny, which was short for Bernice, a name which they'd found in some book. Peta smiled. Bunny wouldn't thank them for such a nickname when she grew up.

As the silent morning slipped away the snow eased off. The men in the neighbourhood began to clear their pathways, so Peta decided to do the same to keep her mind occupied. She donned wellies, a thick old duffle-coat and a woolly hat in bright red to cover her ash-blonde curly hair, and by the time she had heaved away some of the snow her nose and cheeks matched her hat.

'That's no job for a woman.' An unfamiliar masculine voice made her look up curiously, and she stopped shovelling.

She had been about to inform the onlooker that as she had no man to do it for her, it was her job. But how did she know who he was, and could he be trusted? Never wise, her mother had warned, to let on that you were a woman alone.

'Is this number fifty-six?' he asked with a tight smile.

Peta turned and glanced pointedly at the wrought iron numbers by the front door of the glass porch.

'That's what it says.' Her breath came in short gasps and she was glad of a rest, but the tall man before her looked official-like and was surveying her as critically as she was him.

'You wouldn't be Miss Blair, by any chance?' he asked hesitantly, a formidable frown creasing his brow.

Peta hedged. 'Who wants to know?' she asked stonily.

'Ashley Reeves.' He gazed at her as if she ought to recognise the name. 'The new tenant, ground floor flat, I believe. Mr Fitzgerald should have informed you. He meant to bring me along and introduce me personally but I've arrived a day or so early in view of the weather forecasts.'

'Oh.' Peta didn't quite know how to react. 'How d'you do,' she muttered at length. 'I've had the heating on a bit every day to keep the flat aired. It still smells a bit of putty and paint, but I hope you'll find it comfortable.'

'I'm sure I shall, Miss Blair. It's in an ideal spot for my work. Close to the town, too.'

'We have a nice open view at the back, although I suppose I get the best of that from upstairs.' Why was she sounding apologetic! 'Have you come far? I mean, how did you get here? Everything seems to have stopped suddenly.'

'I tried to beat the snow-storm but instead I got caught in it, so my car is left stranded on the dual carriageway a few miles back. The police advised me to walk, but I was lucky, a farmer came along with a tractor and brought me into town. I take it you do have a key, Miss Blair?'

'Ye-es.' Doubts invaded Peta's brain. This wasn't in the letting contract. Mr Fitzgerald had promised she wouldn't be bothered in any way.

'You'll want me to identify myself. I appreciate your mistrust,' he offered with the weeniest hint of sarcasm.

'It's not that I mistrust anyone, Mr—er—Ashley did you say?'

'Ashley Reeves, but Ashley will do very nicely.'

It might for him, she thought, but she intended to keep her distance. It was a business arrangement and Peta had stated that a middle-aged couple would be preferable, people who would treat the house with respect. Her spirits lifted. Perhaps he was just visiting for Christmas.

'You're just here for Christmas, is that it?' she asked hopefully. 'Your family coming later?'

His mid-brown eyes narrowed against the bitter north-east wind, and he seemed to change the weight from first one foot, then the other. His expression clearly defined that he thought she was a dimwit.

She placed the shovel against the wall of the house.

'I'll get the key.'

He fished in his pocket and brought out a letter from Mr Fitzgerald, the estate agent, and with it his passport. Peta glanced briefly after she had fetched the key from the porch and hurried to open his front door, which was adjacent to her own.

'You go on in,' she said. 'I'll take off my wellies and put the kettle on, you must be cold.' When she'd made a huge mug of instant soup and added a good-sized cheese sandwich to the tray, she met him again in the porch.

He smiled and took the tray, saying, 'That's better, and thanks for this, most kind of you. Perhaps you'd better just come in and give me the benefit of your advice on the central heating and how to use the cooker, though I'm sure I can manage.'

She had removed her woollen hat and fluffed up her silky hair. She noticed that his fleecy-lined sheepskin car coat was open and he was trailing a striped university scarf.

'You're lucky to find me in,' she said with a nervous laugh. 'I should have gone to Sussex, but now—' she shrugged.

'You haven't made soup for yourself,' he said, sounding a bit like a schoolmaster.

'No.'

'And you seem to have misheard me, Miss Blair. I am the new tenant. I'm sorry Mr Fitzgerald hasn't given you the full details, I do hope this doesn't mean that you disapprove of letting your flat to a bachelor?'

What could she say? Of course she didn't disapprove, but she had agreed with Ivor and Ros that a middle-aged couple would be most suitable. Or had Ivor and Ros agreed with her? It didn't matter. The point was that she hadn't expected a bachelor. Younger, too, than she'd at first thought.

He had a shock of dark brown, wavy hair, which was in her opinion an inch or so too long at the back of his neck. A wayward lock fell over his forehead at one side, but it suited his longish face. He appeared to be fluttering thick dark lashes as he waited for a reply.

'No, I don't suppose I mind,' she said, 'but you're not quite what I expected.'

He raised one eyebrow in what she considered to be a mocking way, so she hurried through the ground floor flat giving brief explanatory details, and then beat a hasty retreat back upstairs.

It was late afternoon when Ivor managed to get through on the telephone, and to her surprise he didn't press her to try to get to Sussex.

'They say it's going to get warmer tonight in your area and there'll be a thaw, but in forty-eight hours there's more bad weather coming and it sounds as if it'll keep us all housebound. Pet, we really are sorry,' he said with genuine regret, 'but you must think of your job. It would be awful if you got here and couldn't get back.'

'Yes, wouldn't it?' she said. 'Don't worry, Ivor. I'll cope, honestly.'

'We'll keep in touch by phone. Haven't you got a friend you could invite to stay with you? Or perhaps there's someone you could go to. What about the neighbours?'

'I'm sure I'd have no trouble finding someone to take pity on me,' Peta said, 'but I shall go to my favourite place – after Sussex, of course,' she put in, tongue in cheek. 'Back to Gida's.'

'But, Pet, the hospital! That means work,' her brother protested.

'Of the very nicest kind, Ivor. My children won't be lucky enough to be able to go home; really, I feel my place is with them.'

Ivor didn't sound impressed. He rambled on

about keeping the house well heated to avoid getting burst pipes. He went on and on infuriating Peta so that she had no chance to tell him about the new tenant, and she felt relieved when at last he rang off.

Before she prepared a meal Peta telephoned the Senior Nursing Officer and explained about the change of plan, suggesting that perhaps she could take some holiday at New Year, or later when the weather was more suitable.

'You sound anxious to get back to work, Sister Blair,' Margaret Astley-Brown said with a chuckle.

'I am,' Peta agreed enthusiastically. 'There's no better place to be than in hospital at Christmastime.'

'I doubt that our patients would agree, but I know what you mean. Are you coming back tomorrow then?'

'I'd like to.'

'I'm sure Staff Nurse Hunter will be delighted. The Royal Marines are coming up from Plymouth to decorate your wards so she'll be grateful that she doesn't have to be in charge.'

'She'd have coped,' Peta said.

'In her professional capacity, yes, but socially she's not the most confident of girls. Still, you never know, the Royal Marines might change all that.'

Margaret Astley-Brown was not a typical Matron. She looked too young to hold such a position, yet everyone knew that she was older than she looked. It was her radiant smile and ability to understand her staff which endeared her to everyone.

They chatted on a few minutes longer and after

Peta had replaced the receiver she prepared for duty next day. When she was making spaghetti bolognese the thought crossed her mind that she ought to have made enough for two and invited her new tenant to share the meal. But she did nothing about it, even though at odd moments her conscience told her that he was probably downstairs with nothing to eat or drink. He had been carrying a holdall type bag she remembered, so consoled herself that it might have contained some food, and she'd given him soup and a sandwich.·

She felt as if a burden had been lifted from her shoulders knowing that she didn't have to go to Sussex, and next morning she was up early, dressed in warm clothing and high-legged boots to trudge through the packed snow to Gida's hospital about three quarters of a mile away.

Catherine Hunter had already reached the children's block, and was in the office glancing through the night report book when Peta entered.

'Brrr,' Peta greeted, 'there's a slight nip in the air, isn't there?'

'And you're mad enough to want to come to work when you could be at home with your feet up?'

'Not much fun when you're all alone with nothing to do except stand at the window and look at the snow. It came at just the right time for me, Cathy, and for once Ivor didn't try to move heaven and earth to get me to Sussex. He sounded as relieved as me that it's off. I know he considers it his duty to invite me, but I'm sure they'd rather have Christmas on their own, and I prefer to be here.'

'So Matron told me, and I'm not going to argue.

You can deal with these Marines when they come.'

'*I* shall need moral support, so no skiving off and leaving me to it. Oh, it'll be much more fun here than at Ivor's.'

For the next hour or so Peta was caught up with the change-over from the night staff and after the report had been given she went to the babies' ward and proceeded to bath and feed the tiniest patients.

Baby Alexander was suspected of having a digestive problem and after being fed Peta had to nurse the infant, hoping that vomiting in a manner significant to pyloric stenosis did not occur.

Martyn Alexander, Marty for short—Peta wondered why parents bothered to find nice names for children only to shorten them—was now seven weeks old and was a fair haired boy with vivid blue eyes. He looked better this morning, Peta thought, and wondered if everyone wasn't worrying unduly about him. She talked to him and he appeared to be listening as though he understood every word she was saying and would have answered if he'd known how. Was there just the hint of a smile?

'Is this going to be our lucky day, Marty?' she crooned to him. 'Maybe you'll be going home for Christmas after all?'

'That would be the nicest present you could give his parents, Sister.'

Peta hadn't heard masculine footsteps intermingling with the light tread of most of the nurses. She glanced over her shoulder, recognising the consultant paediatrician's voice.

'Good morning, Dr Mandeville.' Peta's smile, a special one she kept exclusively for the middle-aged doctor, faded as another figure moved up to the consultant's side. She felt as if someone had thrown cold water over her. The Ashley person, the new tenant of fifty-six Vandyke Crescent, was surveying her with as much disdain as she was him!

'Little fellow looks a bit more lively this morning, Sister,' Dr Mandeville continued. Then, turning to his companion, 'Suspected pyloric stenosis, but,' and he gazed with fond admiration at Peta, 'looks as if my favourite nursing sister has done a first class job again. Sister, this is Ashley Reeves, joining the team for a few months—Sister Blair,' he added by way of introduction.

Peta swivelled round a bit in her chair and extended her hand quickly when she realised that Ashley Reeves was about to divulge that they had already met.

'How d'you do, Mr Ash—Reeves,' she corrected with a forced smile. Why couldn't she get the darned name right, for goodness' sake? She felt the colour rising in her cheeks at her stupid mistake, and at the fierce grip with which he imprisoned her fingers.

'You're very early this morning,' she said agreeably to Dr Mandeville.

'Off to the Swiss Alps, my dear, in a day or two. Thought you were on holiday too.' He clicked his fingers in mock reproach. 'There—let the cat out of the bag, haven't I?'

'A duty visit to Sussex was the plan, but the weather has cancelled it for me,' she replied, 'and I'm not the slightest bit sorry.'

'Now, now, Pet, that's not the Christmas spirit. Only wish I could take you with me, but my lady-wife might get suspicious. We shall be in on Christmas morning, then we're off on Boxing Day. Thought I'd bring Mr Reeves in as quickly as possible. Give him all the help he needs, Pet. I know I can count on you.' He put his arm round the younger man's shoulder and whispered behind his hand. 'Her name is Peta but we all call her Pet; that's exactly what she is.'

'I know,' Ashley Reeves said. 'She happens to be my landlady and came with the highest references. She warmed me up after my long trek yesterday with soup and a sandwich.'

Peta's cheeks turned crimson. Hearing her good deed spelt out with such clarity sounded terribly mean.

'It wasn't much,' she said, 'but my stocks were low as I had intended to be on my way before lunch.' She didn't need to explain to him that her fridge was stocked to overflowing—just in case of a last minute change in plans, which now she was glad she had made provision for.

'It was most kind of you, Sister,' he said, and she recognised that underlying hint of sarcasm again.

Dr Mandeville was glancing from one to the other with a barely concealed smile. He was a very large man. Tall and broad, with a conspicuous fatherly paunch, but features which were rosy and kind. What little hair he had was silver-grey and toned well with his gentle dove-grey eyes.

Peta was comparing the younger man with the darling of Angelique ward when Marty Alexander decided to attract attention by vomiting copiously all over Peta's waterproof apron. Dr Mandeville placed a consoling hand on her shoulder.

'Seems you were a little premature in your

hopes, Sister,' he said sympathetically, and moved away in earnest conversation with the new surgeon.

Peta tended the babe, quickly dealt with the mess and removed her apron, calling to Cathy to come to her assistance so that she could tidy herself and accompany the consultant on his round.

Dr Mandeville had a way of inclining his head and smiling down at her, which he did now as she joined them in the office.

'Sorry if it was our arrival which upset the young man,' he said. 'What do you consider we should do? Keep a close watch on him over the next week, or send him home for Christmas, then have him back again afterwards?'

'That decision must be yours, Dr Mandeville,' she said grinning, an indication that she wasn't prepared to shoulder such responsibility.

The two doctors had been perusing Marty's notes where every detail was carefully logged.

'Mr Reeves' opinion is slightly different from mine, Sister, so you have the casting vote.'

'But that's not fair,' Peta protested.

'If you were out in the jungle and the only medical advisor available?' he urged.

'Surgery would be out in those circumstances so I'd just have to nurse him along the best way I could,' she answered after a few moments consideration.

'Sister Blair here is a great advocate for surgery only as a last resort, or in cases of emergency,' Dr Mandeville explained. 'So, Sister, it looks as if it's you and me against Mr Reeves.' He glanced in the folder he was holding and rubbed his chin with long, skilful fingers.

'It is Christmas, Dr Mandeville,' Peta said in an imploring tone.

'You're right, my dear. He should be at home—the parents seem sensible people and it is their first child, also his first Christmas. We can't rush it, though. Continue with the medication and keep him in your tender loving care for a further twenty-four hours. If he seems no worse when either I or Mr Reeves come round the day after tomorrow, let's see how the parents cope with him for a week.'

In the next few seconds Mr Ashley Reeves quoted several similar cases he had treated with medication and some on whom surgery had been necessary. He mentioned far-off places like Zaire and Ethiopia, and Peta groaned inwardly. A know-it-all for sure, and wasn't it just her luck to have him living in the downstairs flat!

Oswald Mandeville seemed to be impressed. He listened attentively, but so he did to everyone, and he evidently liked the type of man Ashley Reeves appeared to be. Ashley Reeves, Ashley Reeves, Ashley Reeves, Peta repeated to herself several times silently; she *must* get it right!

The round took some time as each case needed to be discussed and examined carefully, and then Peta served them with coffee before they finally left.

Ashley Reeves had given her a penetrating look with his brown eyes, telling her that he considered she and Dr Mandeville were much too familiar. She felt her body tighten when the senior man placed a hand gently on her waist. The little, light, intimate, yet meaningless, touches she'd enjoyed before now seemed oddly out of place and embarrassed her, so that when they moved off down the long corridor Peta experienced a feeling of relief.

By the time she returned to the babies' ward all the tinies had been bathed and fed. She went through the main ward checking on all the toddlers, then on to the older children who liked her to stop and chat, and before she could get back to her office it was time to supervise lunch.

Cathy went off duty in the early afternoon leaving a newly-qualified nurse to attend to the babies' feeds, which gave Peta time to sit at her desk and catch up with some written work. She'd been there no longer than five or six minutes when a brisk tread echoed down the corridor. She expected it to continue on to some other department, but instead the military-sounding footsteps grew nearer and sounded slightly menacing. It wasn't time for visitors yet—and then the doorway was filled with a great deal of masculinity in uniform. She stared stupidly up at her visitor. He smiled in a way that momentarily took her breath away.

'Sister Blair?' he queried.

'Yes,' Peta managed in a humble voice.

'Lieutenant-Colonel Quentin Reeves. I understand you're expecting us. I've come on ahead of my men to discuss plans to decorate your wards.'

She stood up and although she was a long way off his height she felt she was making much of her five feet five inches.

'It's very kind of you to help us in this way,' she began.

'Not at all, Sister. We must keep up the usual tradition of our unit—and since my brother is a doctor here now we must make a good job of it.'

Yes, of course, the smile, the burnt sienna coloured eyes—looking into them she just hoped there weren't any more surprises in store for her today . . .

CHAPTER TWO

'I EXPECT you've met Ashley by now. He tells me you're his landlady as well. Lucky old Ashley,' Quentin Reeves said.

Peta experienced a confusion of emotions. She knew she ought to be cutting the Colonel down to size. He sounded as if he had taken over Gida's hospital—or was that brother Ashley's role? Who did they think they were!

Indignation languished, though, at the officer's smile. Like his brother's, it was the kind you couldn't ignore. Both men held themselves with dignity, pride, cultivated a slightly severe image, yet somewhere in their features lurked signs of recalcitrant desperado. His eyes gleamed with well-being which infected Peta so that she reciprocated with an easy smile.

'He may not think he is so lucky,' she replied quickly. 'We have met, but only very briefly.'

'Brief, but potent. He was grateful for the soup. The weather seems to have changed everyone's plans. Ash came early and you, I understand, have had to rearrange leave. Rotten luck.'

Peta shrugged. She almost confessed that she really was grateful to the weather, but what was it to him? She put her pen back in her pocket and walked towards the door so that Quentin Reeves moved back a pace.

'I'll show you the wards, though I believe you're

only going to decorate the main ward. We hope our patients will be few, so we bring them all in together if possible.'

He pushed open the swing door and held his arm so that she could pass beneath it.

'What did you have in mind?' she asked him.

His mirth exploded into an open grin which progressed to a deep-throated laugh. 'Keeping it on the job, Sister,' he joked, 'but I can't vouch for the propriety of my lads with so much temptation around. Something about blue dresses, white aprons, and wayward curls struggling to get free of starchy caps which definitely defy the most stringent of rules.'

'My nurses will be much too busy to notice what's going on. They—we all are most grateful not to have to do the job ourselves,' she admitted.

Quentin managed to wrest his eyes away from her face and he looked around the high walls and ceiling of the main ward.

'I'm aware that decorations are dust traps and therefore a hygiene hazard, and we have fire regulations to conform to, so we'll go up as high as possible,' he suggested. 'Bunting and coloured foil streamers; the tree is on its way, and I believe you have baubles and bells—though I hope you'll accept the gifts we shall attach to it.'

'You're very kind. The tree is one thing we do leave up until twelfth night. Various choirs and groups come to sing for the children, and we can expect some emergency admissions, so it's nice to retain an air of festivity after the immediate holiday.'

Peta accompanied him as he strode from one end

of the ward to the other, and decided in the end that her suggestions were being banished—he was a man with ideas of his own.

Finally he said, 'Now all I have to do is wait for my contingent to arrive. Ashley not around, I suppose?'

'I expect he's in the hospital somewhere,' Peta said with a degree of indifference. 'I could always phone around.'

'No, I don't wish to put you to any trouble. He knows where to find me so I imagine he'll look in before we leave this evening.'

'Perhaps you'd like a cup of tea while you're waiting for your colleagues,' she suggested hesitantly, knowing that every nurse on duty was finding an excuse to walk through the ward before disappearing into the sluice, no doubt to pool their opinions of the Marine officer.

Peta found one of the junior nurses in the ward kitchen.

'Tray of tea and biscuits, Nurse Kray, please.'

She returned to her office and sat down at the desk, indicating that her visitor should take the armchair in the corner.

He pulled a notebook from his top pocket. It turned out to be a diary.

'We'll return on December twenty-seven to take them down then, Sister. About the same time suit you?'

'As early as you can manage, please,' she said. 'Visitors other than parents come in between four and six so it would be best if it was all finished by the time they arrive.'

'I thought parents came in to stay with children these days?' Quentin Reeves said.

'Some do for short stays. We have several small rooms down the corridor for those people, but so often mothers have other children at home to care for and can only visit daily.'

'I suppose you'd rather have the children without their parents? I know Ashley's a bit old-fashioned in that respect.'

'Each case is different and has to be assessed on its own merits, but by and large it's a great help to have a sensible mother tending her own child. The child is less fractious for one thing, and washing and feeding is more natural with Mum supervising. It saves a great deal of time, giving us more to spend with the others.'

'Forgive me for being personal, Sister Blair, but you're rather young to be holding such a responsible post, aren't you?'

Peta felt her colour rising at his observation.

'It's experience which counts,' she said quietly as she poured tea which the nurse had brought.

'And I have it on the best authority that you have plenty of that.'

She glanced across at him feeling slightly annoyed. How did he know anything about her, she wondered?

As if he read her mind he added, 'Ash has only recently returned from Africa so it was left to me to find him somewhere to live.' He laughed suddenly. 'Forgive me, but you're not what I expected, certainly not what I gave Ash to understand his landlady would be like. Middle-aged, motherly type who would bang on the floor if he had music on after ten at night—you know the sort of thing?'

One glance at his quixotic expression and Peta

was laughing with him, but she didn't divulge that his brother wasn't what she had expected either.

'What's going on here? I thought you'd come to work, not flirt with the nursing staff, and Sister at that!'

Ashley Reeves had approached the office stealthily. He must have done, Peta decided, as few people could walk the long corridor leading to Angelique ward without being heard, and she had gained plenty of practice at detecting various treads over the past two and a half years.

Now that the two brothers were together, Peta could see that they were identical in features. But whereas the doctor was quite dark-skinned, the Marine officer had a fresher complexion and his eyes were not as brown as Ashley's, but had a tinge of yellow about them.

She felt her colour deepen at the implication that Quentin was flirting with her.

'Hullo, Ash, I hoped you'd make your way here. I was just telling your landlady that she isn't quite what I'd led you to believe.' Quentin stood up and patted Ashley's shoulder. There couldn't even be one inch difference in their heights Peta noticed.

Quentin seemed the most extrovert of the two, though somewhere, hidden in Ashley Reeves' still depths, there was a gremlin disturbing the outward calm dignity of the doctor image.

'I believe Sister Blair was equally disconcerted,' Ashley said with a hint of triumph. 'I'm sure we shall look after one another admirably.'

Peta's smile faded and she opened her mouth to scotch any ideas that he had of being anything more than neighbourly, when Quentin, in his familiar way, intervened by saying, 'At least you've got instant female company, Ash, and when we have a party I'm sure Sister Blair will rally a few of her unattached colleagues.'

At that moment Cathy entered the office.

'On duty, Sister,' she reported. At sight of the two men her cheeks turned instantly pink, which seemed to heighten the shade of her attractive auburn hair.

'Any sign of some lost Royal Marines, Nurse?' Quentin asked quickly, obviously a ploy to deter the embarrassed Cathy from hurrying away.

'They don't look lost to me,' she replied curtly. 'They're all changing into plimsolls in the corridor.'

'Good. That means we can get some action.' Suddenly be became the officer in charge of a specific task, but he shot Peta a warm smile. 'Don't accept too many invitations to parties over Christmas. Ash will have to have a house warming.'

He turned and walked briskly away, his decisive step echoing on the concrete floor. Within minutes it seemed as if a war was being waged at Gida's. The men of the Royal Marines all seemed enormous and set about livening up the children's ward with good heart.

Peta felt she ought to go to supervise. She couldn't imagine what they were going to do in her domain and she did have vivid memories of previous experiences when huge flags had stretched from one end of the ward to the other. She had been Staff Nurse in those far-off days, and could well remember Sister Shave's dilemma, not knowing how to tactfully explain that this was Angelique ward, not a ship to be dressed! It had been a bit overpowering, Peta remembered, but they had survived the few days without upsetting the Royal Navy.

'Any tea to spare, Sister?'

She came back to the present and the realisation that Ashley Reeves was still there.

She lifted the small pot. 'Yes, I'll fetch a cup.'

'I don't want to put you to any trouble,' he said.

When she returned from the kitchen he was sitting in the easy chair which a few moments before his brother had occupied.

She noticed his legs stretched out before him, and his long, narrow feet clad in clean and well-polished black slip-on shoes. He'd tucked his hands in his trouser pockets and she sensed that he was shivering.

'As long as it's hot,' he said. 'Just something to warm me up.'

She wondered then if he was feeling ill so glanced down at him with concern, but met those clear, calculating eyes and realised that he was feeling the cold probably more than most.

'Have you only recently returned to this country, Mr Reeves?' she asked.

When he didn't answer she looked at him again.

'You finally got it right,' he said with a grin. 'Still, that's not surprising now that you've met my brother.' He sighed and stirred his tea thoughtfully.

'How so?' Peta asked.

Ashley shrugged and pursed his lips as if he considered her to be asking a stupid question.

'Once you've met Quentin you don't easily forget—so I'm told.' He sipped his tea. 'Yes, Sister Blair, I have just returned from abroad and find it hellishly cold. Oh, I know it's bad for everyone, but such extremes aren't easy to adjust to. I am very relieved to find that the flat has a gas fire as well as central heating.'

'You can always put the thermostat up if it's not warm enough. Each flat is completely self-contained. I must apologise too, Mr Reeves. I should have asked you if you had bread and milk, things like that, when you arrived.'

'Why should you? I caught you on the hop—the weather caught us all on the hop. Thank goodness the thaw has set in. I expect by the time you go home most of the snow on the main roads will have gone, which leads me to the reason for my visit.'

Peta looked at him quizzically.

'I wondered, if you haven't anything special to do tonight, if you'd be kind enough to take me out to the dual carriageway so that I can rescue my car?' he continued. 'The motoring services have promised to do it, but they're frightfully busy so I may have to wait for days.'

Peta glanced out of the office window but a nearby building blocked her view and it was dark anyway now.

'I'm not off duty until eight o'clock,' she said hesitantly, 'and if it freezes again . . .'

'We'll take it slowly,' he suggested. 'I'll drive out and shadow you back in my own car. It shouldn't be so bad now, but I'd be grateful if I could borrow your spade—just in case.'

'Yes, but . . .'

'You'd rather not bother,' he cut in sharply.

'Oh, it's not that, but I don't use my car much in the bad weather.'

'I won't let you come to any harm, I promise,' he said in a patronising way. 'I don't feel I've been here long enough to ask favours.' Then as she gave him a somewhat withering look he added, 'You're different, you're my landlady.' He smiled briefly, drained his cup and was gone.

Peta felt annoyed. Surely such a mission was unnecessary in this weather? It would have been sensible to leave the job to the experienced motoring services. She had a fleeting vision of getting stuck in some God-forsaken spot, and with Ashley Reeves! Now if it was his brother who was seeking a favour . . .

She felt her nerves tingle at the thought. He had the kind of personality any girl would respond to, and some minutes later when Margaret Astley-Brown visited the children's ward on her evening round, she also responded to Quentin Reeves' charms.

Peta accompanied the Senior Nursing Officer and they complimented the Marines, who had hung colourful bunting high from the ceiling. The tree was in its usual corner position and an array of gaily wrapped parcels were stacked at the foot, which was secured in an enormous barrel. Great clusters of brightly coloured balloons also festooned every corner.

'Sister Blair and her nurses will take you to the dining-room where I've ordered supper for you all,' Margaret Astley-Brown told Quentin Reeves. 'I hope you don't have to rush away. It's nice for my girls to have a little unscheduled excitement and you never know, some of your young men might get an invitation to the next hospital dance.'

It was apparent by Quentin's expression that he assumed he would be entertained by Peta, and she was happy to do so. The more she was in his company the better she liked him, and the dining-room was soon echoing to the sound of merry laughter. Even Cathy seemed to have lost some of her inhibitions and appeared to be getting along well with a rather good-looking young man.

Peta was surprised to find that it was almost ten-thirty when Quentin called his men to order and told them to prepare to leave.

'Are the girls in residence here at the hospital?' he asked with some concern.

'Most of them are in the nurses' home,' she replied.

'And you have transport back to your flat?'

Peta shook her head. 'No, I walked in because of the weather. It seemed silly to take a car out on the road—oh, heavens!' she exclaimed, clapping her hand to her mouth. 'I've just remembered; your brother asked me to take him back to where his car was stranded. I quite forgot. Whatever must he be thinking of me?' she said in vexation.

She started off down the corridor at a rate, and Quentin followed.

'I can send the men on back, and I'll go to help Ashley,' he offered. 'It has thawed a bit today but our jeep will be better at pulling him out if he's stuck. I can't imagine why he didn't remind me.'

They returned to Angelique ward where Peta took off her cap and apron before dressing up in her warm coat, fleecy-lined boots and woolly hat.

'I'll run you home and we'll see what my brother has decided,' Quentin suggested.

'That I'm pretty self-centred and thoughtless,' Peta groaned bitterly.

'I'm sure he'll understand—well, as much as *he'll* ever understand a woman,' Quentin added with a laugh.

Peta paid little attention to anything he was saying. She felt so angry with herself for her lack of consideration, especially when she hadn't fallen over with enthusiasm on his arrival. No doubt Ashley Reeves would believe she had stayed on at Gida's on purpose.

As Quentin escorted her to the car park and his jeep, cheery goodbyes were being exchanged by the young men of the Royal Marines and the nurses.

'Let's see if I can remember the way,' Quentin said as he drove off.

'You've already been to Vandyke Crescent?'

'Of course. I could hardly arrange Ashley's living accommodation without vetting it. Mr Fitzgerald took me there one morning a couple of weeks ago and I was most impressed. Had I known that the landlady was so young and charming I'd have arranged to meet her, too—and there was me imagining you to be a fifty-year-old starchy spinster.'

'Not all fifty-year-old spinsters are starchy,' Peta said.

'Don't tell me you expect to still be a spinster at fifty?'

Peta shrugged. 'Who knows?'

'No one special in your life then at present?' he pursued.

'Not at the moment,' she said, and then she had

to direct him through the side streets towards Vandyke Crescent. When they reached number fifty-six the grey, eery, snow-clad night revealed that the place was in darkness.

'Oh dear,' she said, 'your brother must have got tired of waiting and has gone to bed.'

'I doubt that very much,' Quentin said, walking briskly up the drive. 'Ash has seldom been known to turn in before midnight. Which is the bedroom?'

'The front room.'

Quentin continued up the drive and knocked on any window he passed, then he returned to the front and banged quite hard on the bedroom window.

'No,' he said, 'it's obvious that Ash isn't in. Did he give you any idea where his car was stranded?'

'On the dual carriageway, but how far back I have no idea.'

'Come on, let's go and see if we can find him. Knowing Ashley's stubbornness he's set out on foot.'

As they got back into the jeep he added, 'You know, I find it quite incredible that he should ask your help. He's an obstinate cuss and will go through hell and high water rather than ask anyone a favour. Guess you made an impression on him. Still,' he glanced across at Peta with a saucy grin, 'that's hardly surprising. I hope we're going to be able to see more of each other, Peta.'

In the darkness her eyes sparkled with pleasure as she replied eagerly, 'I'd like that.'

The main roads were clear and the slightly warmer temperatures had turned the surface to wet blackness. Peta needed to hang on to her seat as

Quentin drove at a rather reckless speed, the tyres frequently screeching as he went round bends and corners too fast.

They had reached the edge of town and had turned to go up the hill towards the roundabout when a tall figure loomed ahead of them, briskly striding it out.

'There he is—that's got to be Ashley. As always, doing his thing perfectly, wearing a light raincoat so that he can be picked out easily and walking towards oncoming traffic.'

'How can you be so sure?' Peta said. 'It could be anyone.'

Quentin laughed and sounded the horn as he overtook the walker before pulling in on to the grass verge.

Peta half turned to look over Quentin's shoulder and saw with some relief that it was indeed Ashley Reeves. He took his time crossing the road and then he stood at Quentin's window.

'What are you doing on this road?' Then peering in and seeing that Quentin had company he stopped abruptly. 'Oh—'

'We're looking for you,' Quentin said. 'Come on, Ash, get in and let's go to find your car before the next blizzard obliterates it.'

'Shouldn't you be on your way to Plymouth?'

'Yes, I should, but I do happen to be the commanding officer, and I can catch my men up, I expect.'

Ashley walked round the front of the vehicle and opened the door. The jeep had a front bench seat with similar arrangements along the sides in the rear.

'So it's you!' he said with a hint of aggression as he pulled himself up, and Peta found herself packed tightly between the two brothers on the front seat. Quentin sped off again in earnest and at the roundabout Peta was thrown from one to the other as Ashley directed his brother to the right road.

'I really am sorry, Mr Reeves,' she apologised when at last she could get her breath. 'I would have been home ages ago, I don't usually have supper at the hospital, but your brother and his men—'

'Don't apologise, Sister Blair,' he cut in shortly. 'Wherever Quentin goes he takes command of everyone and every situation.'

'That's not true, Ash,' Quentin denied indignantly. 'The Matron invited us all to have supper before we started back, and Peta was detailed to look after me.'

'How very convenient for you,' Ashley said sarcastically.

It was clear to Peta that there was some animosity between the two men though Quentin, in his easy-going, friendly manner, was anxious to hide it.

'Can you remember exactly where your car is?' she asked the surgeon in an effort to be congenial.

'Of course,' came the cryptic reply. '*I* have an excellent memory.'

Peta fell silent, her cheeks flushing in spite of the cold wind that came into the jeep from every angle. She knew that he was insinuating that she had forgotten about his request for help. She couldn't honestly deny it, but she had apologised—what more could she do? It was lucky for him that his brother was willing to give up his time to go to his aid.

'What type of car is it?' Quentin asked.

'Granada.'

'Very nice too. What about yours, Peta?'

She laughed. 'Just a humble Ford Escort,' she said.

'An admirable choice,' Ashley said. 'They're economical and reliable usually. They're used abroad a great deal and seldom let us down.'

'Glad to be out of the jungle and back to civilisation, Ash?' Quentin asked.

'I'm not wildly enthusiastic about this weather,' he admitted, 'but it's good to be home.'

'Seen the parents?'

'Briefly.'

'Did you have to start work immediately? Couldn't you have spent Christmas with them?' Quentin asked.

'I would have done had they been spending it at home, but they've flown to Tenerife.'

'Why didn't you go there too? It would have made a nice stop-over, and relieved the pressure of two such extreme climates, I would have thought,' Quentin suggested.

Ashley didn't react at once, but Peta could feel his muscles tighten. She noticed that he had clenched his fists into tight balls between his knees. Then, between gritted teeth, he said, 'Why the inquisition? Am I cramping your style? I decided it was better to get settled in close to the hospital as quickly as possible in view of the time of year, and appreciating that Dr Mandeville was due to go on holiday.'

'Sorry,' Quentin said in a contrite voice.

They must have travelled some four or five miles before a snow plough came into view, and behind it several cars were lined up in a lay-by.

'Pull in over there,' Ashley ordered and Quentin did so.

There was almost no traffic on the road now, and spaces between the stranded cars indicated that some owners had been earlier in the day to rescue vehicles.

Ashley was out of the jeep and had unlocked his car before the sound of the jeep's engine faded. Quentin glanced across at Peta and raised his eyebrows.

'You're thinking you've never met twin brothers so unalike?' he asked with a grin.

'*Twin* brothers?' Peta echoed in surprise. 'There are physical similarities if you look hard enough,' she began.

Quentin placed a hand on her knee. 'If you've looked *that* hard it must mean you're interested. But in which one of us? Dare I hope?'

Peta could only just make out his features in profile but she knew he was smiling in an honest way. He was so easy, so warm a personality that she automatically responded with an equally friendly smile.

'I had to take an interest in your brother,' she whispered conspiratorially, 'because we have to work together. He takes life rather more seriously than you, I imagine, so he's not so easy to get to know. Whatever made him go abroad to work? By odd remarks it sounds as if he's been away a long time.'

Peta sensed that even Quentin raised a barrier against this observation.

'You must ask him all about Africa,' he said quietly, then opened his door and jumped down.

Peta decided to stay in comparative shelter until the men had started up the car, but when she took a closer look she noticed windscreen wipers going and puffs of exhaust being carried away in the cold night air. As she listened she could hear the low murmur of the smoothly-running engine beneath the brothers' voices.

It seemed that they were talking confidentially as they moved round to the offside of Ashley's Granada, their backs protected from the wind by the high country hedge.

Peta decided to remain where she was and, although curious as to the tone of their conversation, she only occasionally caught an odd word when voices were raised.

It seemed ages before they began to saunter back to the jeep and Quentin opened the passenger door.

'Is everything all right?' Peta asked anxiously.

'With a car like that you could leave it out on the moors for a decade and it would still start first time. For once Ashley's invested in a sensible car,' Quentin said.

'Let's hope the driver is as reliable.' There it was again, such sarcasm, but who was it aimed towards? Himself or his brother, or perhaps someone who had come between them at some time?

'Ashley will take you home, Peta,' Quentin said, holding out his hand to help her down. 'I can then stay on the dual carriageway and catch up with my lads.'

'Do take care,' she advised solemnly, 'it must be near freezing again and you might suddenly hit an icy patch.'

As she stood beside him she was dwarfed between him and Ashley. Quentin still held her arm and suddenly bent to kiss her in a polite, social way.

'Thanks for your concern. I'll take care just so that I can see you again quite soon.'

He walked to Ashley's car with her and she sat in it securing her safety belt, with strange misgivings. She didn't feel at ease with Ashley and she wished Quentin was taking her home.

The brothers shook hands as they parted, and as Ashley took his place behind the steering-wheel she could feel his resentment smouldering beneath the surface. He certainly had a chip on his shoulder about something—and yet when he had first arrived at Vandyke Crescent he'd been pleasant enough, she remembered.

As they drove home in total silence she tried to pinpoint when he had changed. Perhaps he hadn't though. When he first arrived at Vandyke Crescent he might have been putting on an act of conviviality to impress his landlady. Most doctors, especially those who had risen to consultant level, had a distinctive manner but Peta, after much thought, came to the conclusion that the 'chip' had appeared most noticeably when he was in the company of his brother.

'Are you on duty early tomorrow?'

Peta, although deep in thought in connection with Ashley Reeves, was moved by the softness of his tone, and she glanced across at him as if to remind herself which brother was driving.

'No, thank goodness, I'm on late turn.'

'Good, that means that we can both sleep on.'

As he turned into the driveway of number fifty-six he actually chuckled. 'You in your small corner and I in mine,' he said pointedly.

CHAPTER THREE

PERHAPS he wasn't so bad after all, she reflected as she fitted her key into the lock. She'd opened up the double garage and switched the light on for him before going to her front door and as she went inside snapped on the porch light as well. She heard the up and over garage door close while she was pulling off her boots, and seconds later Ashley stood in the porch.

'Everything all right?' he asked as he jingled his bunch of keys.

'Fine,' she answered. 'Thanks for the lift home.'

'My pleasure, though I'm a poor substitute for my brother. There's not room for two of us in the same spot at the same time, as you'll discover.' He opened his door, disappeared, then put his head inside her door again. 'Your key. I went to see the agent during my lunch-time so I'm legally installed now. You'll need it to check on your tenant from time to time.'

His dark eyes were quite brazenly flirting with her.

'I'll hang it here just in case of emergency,' she said, taking the spare key. Then, feeling flustered, she added, 'I suppose you'd like a hot drink?' Now why had she said that? She recognised such patronage in her own voice and wished she could retract the offer.

'I would indeed,' he agreed, 'and so would you, but this time be *my* guest.'

'It . . . it's rather late, isn't it?'

He cocked an eyebrow knowingly. 'It is, but do we have anyone to consider but ourselves; each other?' he queried.

'I'll just nip up and put my electric blanket on,' she said. 'Do you have coffee and milk?'

'Everything we need,' he stated. 'Come in when you're ready.'

She couldn't imagine why she needed to comb her hair and apply fresh make-up at this hour. Perhaps to gain time and confidence?

After a brief tap on the door she pushed it open, went inside and closed it firmly. The ground floor flat smelt warm and she appreciated that Ashley needed to keep the heating on at a highish temperature to counteract having come from a much warmer part of the world. In a few moments her cheeks were glowing.

He appeared at the kitchen door and indicated that she should go in to the lounge.

'Make yourself at home,' he offered. 'But, of course, this is your home.'

Peta sat as far as she could from the gas fire which was burning, giving the room extra warmth as well as a welcome cosiness from the brightly lit log effect. It gave her a pang of emotion being downstairs again, and the room still seemed to live and breathe of a happy family. She looked down at the carpet near the patio doors covered by thick lined curtains, where she half-expected to see her father's slippers. Her glance moved to the big easy chair by the fireplace and she felt her mother's presence.

It was Christmas, Peta's first without some member of her own family, and she experienced an odd twinge of despair as Ashley wheeled a trolley into the room. She was in a strange room with a strange person, she reminded herself, but as he poured coffee from a shiny new percolator and asked if she took milk and sugar his dark eye reflected a look of understanding.

'Have you everything you need?' she enquired politely, realising that as landlady she had certain obligations to fulfil.

He sat down in her mother's chair close to the fire.

'Pretty well,' he replied. 'It's a very comfortable flat and I'm grateful for the instant warmth. Naturally I shall discover personal things I need as time goes by, but we all make our own dwelling-place into a home. That isn't to say that I don't feel this is home.' He smiled across at her with a directness which brought an unrecognisable feeling inside her. 'It's been a happy home for its occupants. Perhaps it's been a shattering experience for you to have to give up half of it, Peta,' he said compassionately.

'I just hope you'll be happy here,' she said softly, trying not to give too much of her true feelings away.

'I'm sure I shall, but I want you to be happy to have me, my dear. Changes in life are inevitable, and it takes time to readjust. Mr Fitzgerald has explained the circumstances. I believe your brother was eager to sell?'

Peta's head jerked up defiantly.

'Only because he realised that I couldn't finance a house this size on my own. I couldn't bear to sell though. I know I couldn't be happy living anywhere else.'

'It's rare to meet a home-bird these days. Every-one wants to travel and explore. Well,' he shrugged, 'it's so easy, isn't it?'

'For some,' she said solemnly. 'I just like it right here. What took you to Africa, Mr Reeves?'

'Oh, come on, Peta.' He laughed suddenly. 'I may not have the ready charm and wit that Quentin has, but I'm not that much of a bore am I? Ashley, please. We're both old enough and experienced enough to know that Christian names aren't per-mitted on the wards, but if your chief consultant can call you Pet, can't I?'

He arched his eyebrow mischievously so that she was forced to respond with a shy smile. 'Call me what you like,' she said.

'Peta,' he said, as much to himself as addressing her. 'You mentioned that I wasn't what you were expecting. Does that mean that you'd have prefer-red one of your colleagues to share with you? Another Sister perhaps?'

'No,' she said positively. 'On the contrary. We thought –' Who thought? Who had made the deci-sions? Ivor and Ros? Or was this how she wanted things to be?

'I mean,' she went on hesitantly, 'it didn't seem a good idea to have anyone connected with the hos-pital. I know the flats are self-contained, but I'd imagined a middle-aged couple.'

'Mm, I'm sorry, no wonder I came as something of a shock.'

'It really doesn't matter. Evidently Mr Fitzgerald thought you were suitable, and you're here now, so –'

'You won't turn me out?' In his twinkling eyes

she saw something of Quentin. Perhaps they were more alike than they realised.

'That side of it is left strictly to the agent,' she said. 'We decided it was best that way.'

'We?'

'My brother and his wife. I should have gone to spend Christmas with them.'

'I reckon you'd have got through today. I know they forecast more snow, but traffic is on the move at present.'

'I can't mess them about. I changed plans so I shall stay now. I can always visit them later on.'

'You have plenty of friends I expect?'

Peta nodded. 'Hospital life is good at Christmas.'

'I know, that's why I was glad of the excuse to come on early.'

'Rather than go to Tenerife?' she quipped.

His face clouded and he stared unseeingly into his coffee cup. Then, remembering she was there, he glanced at her with a meaningless smile.

'I've had enough of foreign countries for a while.'

Peta sensed that she had stirred memories. He seemed reluctant to talk about Africa, she'd noticed, and by the silence which ensued she recognised that he needed to be alone so she finished her coffee and stood up.

'It's late,' she said. 'I hope Quentin caught up with his men.'

Ashley got to his feet too. 'I'm sure he did. Forgive me if I'm not quite the scintillating company my brother is. It's the social life they lead, you know. But it's all on the surface. Don't be misled by his attention, Peta. I suppose some would say that servicemen are fickle, and it's innocent people who get hurt.'

'Quentin doesn't seem the type to hurt anyone. He was at Gida's to do us a favour and we're most grateful. We can't make up to the children completely for being away from home during what must be the most important time in a child's life, but we can do our best.'

Ashley dug his hands deep into his pockets and escorted her to the door. He waited until she was inside her own flat, then with a nod he wished her good night and they each closed their respective front doors.

As she cleansed her face, removing all traces of make-up, Peta pondered over recent events. Quentin Reeves was certainly more extrovert than Ashley, but even he lost some of his inhibitions when he was apart from his brother. She wondered why this should be. He was a competent surgeon, and in dealing with children should have lost all traces of reticence by now. Had something occurred in the past which had forced a rift?

There was nothing in Quentin's behaviour to suggest that he was anything but devoted to his twin. It all seemed to be on Ashley's side. It was as if he was trying to keep some aggression at bay when in the company of Quentin. He was quick to react sarcastically, and now he had hinted that his brother was unreliable. In his involvement with women, she assumed he meant. Had he been warning her not to get involved? Why should she listen to him? She realised how much Quentin had impressed her and instead of her last thoughts being of her beloved Dr Mandeville they were of Quentin.

Although Peta was glad of the opportunity to sleep on for an hour next morning, she left her flat allowing plenty of time to walk to Gida's. On her way she bought a paper and called in to the dairy to have her order continued again, as well as collecting bits of shopping for old Mrs Hubbard and Mr Collins who lived on the corner.

It was bitterly cold and she shuddered as she glanced up at the thickening grey sky. Within forty-eight hours the blizzard was supposed to hit them and she was thankful to be on home ground. She promised herself she would have more time to chat to Vandyke Crescent's elderly folk on her return this evening, but soon someone had to make a decision about Baby Alexander. As she hurried along she wondered if Dr Mandeville, affectionately known among the staff as Ossy, would visit Angelique ward today. And would Ashley be with him?

It was a long time, she reflected, since another man had taken precedence in her thoughts over the senior consultant paediatrician, and now there were two of them! Her love and admiration for Ossy was something she kept to herself. They were feelings which had grown over the past two and a half years out of mutual caring for the children who came under their supervision.

Peta suspected some of her colleagues talked about her behind her back, perhaps even more so since the news that Ossy's wife had a particularly nasty type of incurable cancer had leaked eight months ago. They were a devoted couple but childless, so that Ossy and his wife were generous benefactors to Angelique ward.

Peta was often invited to parties at the consultant's house; she suspected Ossy of trying to pair her off with a variety of younger doctors in the past but for a few months now she had not seen Mrs Mandeville. The news that they were going abroad immediately after Christmas was good though, and Peta looked forward to seeing the consultant's wife on Christmas Day.

As she walked up to the entrance of Gida's a large, bronze-coloured car, which she recognised as Ashley's, swept past her, and before she had crossed the hall toward the stairs he caught up with her.

'Foolish girl,' he reprimanded. 'You could have come in with me. I watched for you, heard your door close, then you seemed to have disappeared off the face of the earth.'

'I called to see if there was anything Mrs Hubbard wanted, also Mr Collins,' she explained. 'They live alone so I keep an eye out, though they both have home helps and meals on wheels. But that's not every day, of course. I like walking anyway; thanks all the same.'

'Independent to a fault,' he commented drily and went off in another direction.

This was just what Peta had wanted to avoid. A tenant who would watch her every move. Someone who knew too much about her, felt they had an obligation towards her and from who she would have few secrets. She failed to understand and was peeved that the agent, Mr Fitzgerald had either misunderstood or deliberately misinterpreted her suggestions regarding a suitable tenant for the ground floor flat. She had foreseen a middle-aged couple, people who were self-sufficient, probably with family involvement so that they wouldn't need to show any interest in their landlady.

She supposed that at nearly twenty-five she was a bit young to be a landlady, and whoever rented the flat, short of a girl of her own age, might feel she needed mothering. She hadn't bargained on a bachelor though, and one who was to work closely with her.

Bother Mr Fitzgerald, she thought crossly, as she walked through the long corridors at Gida's. He'd taken too much upon himself and she would have to tell him so when she next met him.

On top of that there was Quentin. He was disturbing in the extreme. She was trying not to make anything of his obvious attraction towards her. She'd been in hospital life long enough to have learnt that you simply didn't react to every pass which was made at you. Nurses were in such a vulnerable position, but they were supposed to be able to control their emotions, she told herself with mild rebuke. I'm only human, she argued silently, and she did genuinely like Quentin Reeves, but that twin brother was something else to be reckoned with. He disturbed her too, but that, she decided, was all to do with being a doctor at Gida's and her tenant. The type of tenant she could well have done without.

The office on Angelique ward was empty when she arrived, so she hung her coat on the hanger at the back of the door and changed her fur-lined boots for her duty shoes. Sensible mid-heel, T-bar leather shoes which had cost the earth, but were comfortable. She was fastening her black belt over her clean white apron when Night Sister joined her.

'Morning, Peta. What's it like out on this dreary winter morning?'

'Cold and messy underfoot. It's been raining, that kind of sticky drizzle wich will eventually turn to snow I fancy.'

'It's being so cheerful that keeps you going I suppose!' Nicola Terry quipped.

'Better to be prepared, and the forecast is a blizzard unless it changes direction. Anyway, what's wrong with snow at Christmas-time? It's the proper time to have it.'

Nicola half grunted, half laughed. 'Just because it happens to suit you doesn't mean it pleases everyone. Can't understand you wanting to be on duty all over Christmas. Still, I suppose a kiss from Ossy under the mistletoe is better than any brotherly affection.'

'Bother,' Peta exclaimed. 'I'd forgotten about mistletoe. I meant to buy some.'

'Pull the other one, Sister Blair. What you mean is that you're one of the lucky ones who can do without it. I can't understand why you're not married.' Nicky, a girl of twenty-eight, about the same height as Peta but skinny to the point of being shapeless, sat down impatiently at the desk and surveyed her colleague with envy in her small, pale green eyes. 'I don't even know how you managed to get to the Finals stage. You *must* have had lots of opportunities, Peta?'

'We all got some,' Peta retorted, 'the few I had came at the wrong time, I suppose.'

'Such as?' Nicky urged.

'Well,' Peta said, settling her cap, with its attractive frilled edge, on her short fair hair before perching on the corner of her desk, 'there was this black American doctor who wanted me to go to Peru with him to do research.'

'Research into what?' Nicky's eyebrows almost left her forehead.

Both girls laughed, then Peta said, 'No, I'm serious. He was really a rather splendid man. Martin Luther King and Sydney Poitier all rolled into one. He wasn't looking for marriage, just companionship.'

She took a photograph out of her handbag. 'There, that's Cornelius – we still correspond.'

'How could you bear to let him go?' Nicky enthused.

'I didn't want to go somewhere so remote and I can't imagine what brother Ivor would have said. Maybe I'm resigned to being a spinster because Ivor once predicted I would be – in the heat of a family row many years ago. I suppose I was a crazy romantic kid in those days, fancying myself travelling and doing exciting things, and here I am perfectly content to stay put and be sister of a children's ward,' she concluded, revealing things she had never told her colleagues at Gida's before.

'You're a dark horse,' Nicky said. 'I only wish I'd got more time to listen to you spinning yarns but I haven't even started the report yet.'

'It's all true,' Peta said wistfully, swinging her legs. 'One or two more down to earth opportunities arose when I was looking after my parents, but as soon as a fella realises you've got commitments within the family he loses interest.'

'Don't I know it,' Nicky sighed.

'How is your Mum, Nicky?' Peta asked with genuine concern.

'She's all right, really. Since the shop-lifting episode was brought out into the open she seems less moody. She's still having treatment and it is working.' Nicky twirled her pen between her fingers thoughtfully. 'It's poor old Dad I feel sorry for. He says he understands, but I see him watching her and frequently offering to do the shopping. He even suggested early retirement; that might come soon enough but I know he feels obliged to keep tabs on Mum. That's why I chose to do nights, it gives me time during the day to keep Mum company, but it isn't exactly conducive to one's social life. Thought I'd have a party just after Christmas though. You'll come, won't you?'

'I'd love to, Nicky. It'll do your Mum good. They ought to get away for a real holiday in the spring.'

'That's just what I told them, so you back me up.' Nicky's expression had grown more relaxed as she'd talked to Peta, who knew and understood about her home pressures. Suddenly Nicky stood up, her face a study in sobriety. 'Good morning, Mr Reeves.'

Peta jumped off the desk as Ashley Reeves walked into the office.

'Don't let me disturb the girl-talk,' he said with a measure of sarcasm, 'but I believe you have a new admission for me. Fractured skull?'

'Yes, he was brought in late last night,' Nicky explained.

'So why wasn't I sent for late last night?'

Nicky looked puzzled. She wasn't used to such direct hostility. Like Peta she was well qualified, and in this instance had agreed with the houseman that bed-rest was the only treatment for the present.

'We don't—' she began.

'Well do so in future. Now that you're both here together it gives me the opportunity to tell you that day or night I wish to be informed of new admissions in serious conditions. Take me to him, Sister.'

'I'll go, Nicky,' Peta offered. 'I'm on duty now and you still haven't done your report.'

'Then you shouldn't be wasting time chatting, surely? I'd rather Night Sister tells me about him, thank you, Sister Blair.'

Ashley Reeves' rebuff was so sharp that neither girl was able to retaliate and Peta could only stand and watch indignantly as Nicky led the way to the small side ward where a young boy of about nine years old was being specialled by a second year nurse, his general condition being carefully monitored constantly.

Peta went into the babies' ward and gradually the day staff reported for duty and intermingled with the night staff for the last half hour of their tour on duty.

There was bed-making to supervise and a medicine round to do before the babies needed to be bathed and fed, but Peta was anxious to know how Marty Alexander and Gary Llewellyn were this morning.

Staff Nurse Cathy Hunter was already perusing Marty's fluid chart.

'Mm,' she murmured handing the clip-board to Peta, 'no copious vomiting overnight.'

'Hopeful—but then I've said that before and he's

reacted to the contrary. Somehow though, I think he needs quiet and patience when feeding. I wonder if his Mum hurries him too much and passes on her agitation? I'm going to be tied up with this new admission, so I'd like you to deal with Marty this morning and take your time.'

Peta glanced at the sleeping Marty before leaning over the side of the next cot where Gary Llewellyn was kicking happily and looking less flushed.

'You're going home for Christmas, young man,' she said in a friendly tone to which he answered with gurgling smiles. 'He's responded excellently,' she said to Cathy. 'Temperature down and keeping steady, and his chest sounds clear now.'

They were moving on to an eighteen month old boy who had a fractured femur so both limbs were suspended vertically to a beam above his cot.

'Wish I could say the same for you, David, but you'll need to stay put for a couple more weeks.' She paused to talk to him and had moved on into the main ward and was chatting to Stephanie, a frail, golden-haired child of seven who was in for blood tests, when Nicky hurried into the ward.

Peta noticed that she looked irritated and ready to explode.

'Mr Reeves is organising an immediate brain scan on Paul Newton,' she said, then in a low voice added, 'Can't see him getting on with Ossy. He's so—so self-opinionated.'

'Early days yet,' Peta said trying to soothe her colleague. 'We'll have to show him that we're quite satisfied with the way he runs things here at Gida's.

Just because he's travelled the world he thinks he knows everything.'

'Thank goodness we're not too full,' Nicky sighed. 'The report won't take me too long, so if you don't mind I'll get on with it.'

Peta went to the side ward where Paul Newton was lying in a semi-conscious state and took over from the nurse. She endeavoured to reassure his anxious parents and later she left him in the capable hands of the scanner technician. No sooner had she returned to the ward than the telephone started ringing.

A child of eight had trapped her fingers in the hinge side of a door and was being admitted from Casualty, and before the morning was through she heard that two young boys were also to be admitted with fractures following a tobogganing accident.

'Why aren't they going to the Orthopaedic Unit?' Peta asked.

'Because they don't have any room, and we thought you'd like the children for Christmas. Compound fractures both of them, so no hope of going home now. You can't complain, Pet, you did choose to work over Christmas so we may as well make it worth your while,' houseman Craig Murray teased. 'I'll make it up to you,' he added. 'Don't worry about mistletoe, we'll manage without; your place or mine?'

'Keep your mind on your work,' Peta quipped light-heartedly, 'we're too busy to think about such things.'

'You're coming to the houseman's party though on Christmas Day, aren't you?'

Peta laughed. 'Not if your reputation is anything to go by,' she said.

'Ah, intrigued, aren't you? So you'll come to find out for yourself.'

Peta was still smiling to herself when Ashley Reeves walked briskly into her office.

'The boy back yet?' he asked. Then, noticing her expression of amusement, he asked, 'What's tickled you?'

She didn't know why she flushed or why she connected the word mistletoe with the new doctor.

'Nothing,' she replied vaguely, 'and no, Paul isn't back yet. Shall I bleep you as soon as I get the message?'

'No, I'll go there now.' It seemed as if he might leave at once, but he paused. Then moving closer, he pulled her ear gently as he said, 'Can't you share the joke?'

Peta was a little taken aback by his gesture, especially as he had seemed to be much less than easy-going earlier. She shook her head. 'No, couldn't possibly,' and she turned her attention to the off duty rota she was preparing.

He murmured something which Peta didn't catch as he vacated her office and moments later the porters arrived with the new admissions from casualty.

It was lunch-time soon and after that some of the nurses went off duty, but somehow they coped throughout the afternoon and while visitors helped the children with tea, Peta concentrated on ordering supplies from the CSSD.

As always, gifts had arrived in great quantities—from the single home-made cuddly toy to box-loads of games and puzzles. The nurses had spent every spare minute making jumbo-sized net stockings and before they went off duty Peta and Cathy had to allot the toys to individual children, remembering to keep some aside for any last minute newcomers.

'It's rotten for the kids who have to stay in hospital over Christmas, and their families,' Cathy said. 'It must mess up the entire Christmas for the parents as well as brothers and sisters.'

'But their loss is our gain,' Peta said, securing a big blue bow on a brown bear which she had singled out for Marty Alexander. 'I wonder if Marty will go home at the last moment.'

'You're rotten,' Cathy said with a knowing grin. 'You don't want him to.'

'Guess he's kind of special,' Peta said, 'but I know his parents ought to have him. Won't seem the same without him.'

'Mr Reeves wants to operate.'

'Has he said so?'

'Not in so many words.'

'Ossy knows what I think,' Peta said defiantly.

'And Ossy will listen to you,' Cathy answered with a grin.

'It can wait until after Christmas,' Peta said solemnly.

At last Peta wrote her report and went off duty much later than her scheduled time, just as the blizzard swept across Dartmoor and up country. She was glad to get home after delivering the shopping to her elderly neighbours and decided against trying the engine of the old family car which she had hung on to. She wouldn't be able to drive anyway if the snow settled and the news, which she watched while eating, forecast the worst possible conditions.

The wind was soon howling round the house. She hung up a few decorations now that she knew she was staying home, and put up a small imitation tree which she covered with baubles and tinsel. Then she soaked in a hot bath and was in the middle of washing her hair when the lights went out.

For a few seconds panic seized her, but she continued under the shower rinsing away all the soap and then, draped in towels, she groped her way into the lounge, thankful that she always kept matches on the mantelpiece for her gas fire.

As she lit the fire she tried not to think about the freezer. The electricity was bound to come on at any moment—but as the minutes ticked away, total darkness prevailed.

In spite of the cold she pulled back the curtains everywhere so that the snow reflected some light inside. When she was clad in warm pyjamas and a velour wrap-around dressing-gown, she found some candles which she kept in a kitchen cupboard, left there from the last electricity cut which must have been when her mother was alive.

Without electricity she had no means of drying her hair except by sitting close to the gas fire and rubbing vigorously. She wished she had batteries for the radio; now she realised how hopelessly dependent she was on electricity. It seemed eery and still—and then suddenly her front door bell broke the silence.

Carol singers, she thought, no need to answer the door. But after a moment's contemplation she wondered who would be out on a night like this. Mrs Hubbard perhaps? Or Mr Collins needing help?

She opened the door at the top of the stairs and with the aid of a torch cautiously went down to the front door.

'Who is it?' she called.

The letterbox rattled and two fingers appeared.

'It's me, Peta. Ashley. Are you all right?'

'Yes, of course. I was just going to bed.'

'Can't you open the door?' he said impatiently. 'I'm on the scrounge.'

'Well . . .' she began hesitantly, then with a sigh slid back the bolts and he pushed his way inside, closing the door behind him.

In the dim glow from the torch Peta saw his eyes rake over her.

'Sorry,' he muttered in a low voice. 'I just wanted to make sure you were okay, and—um—wondered if you happen to have a spare candle?'

Peta turned and, picking up the hem of her robe, said, 'You'd better come up.'

It wasn't on—it simply wasn't on she thought aggressively. Never a minute's peace was she going to get from her bachelor tenant. Mr Fitzgerald was in for a large slice of tongue pie when she next saw him!

CHAPTER FOUR

PETA KNEW that she was showing her irritability in the way she dashed up the stairs and pushed open the saloon-styled kitchen doors. Ashley quickly came up behind her and held the torch while she searched in the cupboard for the new box of candles she knew was there somewhere.

'I'm sorry, Peta,' Ashley said softly. 'I realise I've called at a most inconvenient time. I'll manage—*somehow*.'

'It's all right,' she snapped, 'I know there's a new box here; Mother bought them. I was tempted to throw them away when I had all the sorting out to do, but Mother usually kept a dozen of everything in order to help Mrs Hubbard, and anyone else in need in the road.'

She pulled an assortment of seldom used items out on to the floor. Lavender furniture polish, plate powder for cleaning silver, a box of starch, and a bottle of window cleaner which Ashley picked up and studied calmly.

'Didn't know this, and a few of your treasures there, still existed,' he said in an amused tone.

'It doesn't, anywhere but in Vandyke Crescent,' she answered shortly. She almost disappeared into the cupboard to retrieve a fair-sized box which was right at the back. 'Ah—I knew they were still here. And some night lights as well.'

She stood up and stretched to relieve the pressure on her calves, and was aware of Ashley peering into her face.

'Bit of a hoarder are you?' he asked with a grin.

Peta hesitated, finally calming her fraught nerves. 'A sentimentalist, I suppose. I know I shall never use old-fashioned starch, or lavender polish, but they were things Mother set such store by, so I just couldn't bring myself to throw them away.'

Ashley pinched her chin playfully.

'I like starched pillowcases and the smell of freshly polished furniture, so you never know if I'll come on the scrounge again. I'm glad you found the candles. If we're in for a long siege you'll be glad of them. I'll put them on my shopping list so that we can supply all Vandyke Crescent if necessary.'

'I'm sure it won't be,' she assured him. 'Take the box, I'll try to get some more tomorrow but there'll be a rush on them now, I suppose.'

'No need. Why should you? It's my job to replace what I borrow, and for the record, Peta, this isn't the way I intended to behave. Generally speaking, I'm quite prepared to go without what I haven't got. I do have a hurricane lamp downstairs. I'll admit I came up chiefly to check that you were okay.'

'You mean you've had me turning my cupboards out unnecessarily at this time of night?' she shrieked. She put the box of candles down on the work top with a slam, then knelt to replace all the other items.

'Hurricane lamps need oil, darling, and I'm nearly out of that as well. In any case, candles are more romantic, don't you think?'

'No, not at this moment,' Peta retorted.

'Dinner by candlelight? Oh, come on, Peta, where's the festive spirit in your veins? We all have a yen for the nostalgia of yester year.' He sighed, and helped her up from her knees. 'After being in a completely different climate I'm finding the prospect of a white Christmas quite romantic.'

'How can you feel romantic if you're freezing cold?' she asked on a high note of disbelief.

'Physically cold, yes,' he agreed. 'But that has nothing to do with nostalgia and romance—or the temperature of my heart.'

Peta looked away. She heard him shake the box of candles. 'I'll just take a couple to tide me over,' he said.

'Take what you want,' she replied. 'I've got several.' Then, after a pause, 'Would you like coffee, or tea—or even soup?'

'I thought you'd never ask.'

Peta rounded on him with an aggressive retort bursting from her lips, but the broad smile on his face silenced her.

'Well, which?' she snapped, but managing to add a hint of good humour to her question.

'Which ever you would normally be having—or which ever is easiest.'

'Instant coffee then.'

Ashley placed candles on saucers, and between them they prepared light refreshments which he carried into Peta's lounge. She quickly forgot her annoyance of earlier and was quite glad to have his company. Ashley sat close to the gas fire while Peta tucked her legs beneath her on the matching armchair across the room, with the coffee table between them. The cosy warmth and the dancing shadows from the flickering candle flames dispelled any strain there had been between them.

'I can't really believe you'd rather be here, in this weather, than in Africa,' Peta ventured.

'You can have too much of the sun,' Ashley said with a slow smile. 'It can be unbearable, especially when it contributes to disease. At least there are no flies in England at Christmas time.'

'Were you working in a town hospital or out in the jungle?'

'I did a spell in each. For a while in a large city hospital in Johannesburg, but the greatest need is among children from the poorer villages. I was part of a mobile unit team. It's difficult to believe that such conditions exist when you're in a comfortable place like England.'

'Comfortable?' Peta queried. 'In a blizzard, with no electricity!'

Ashley responded to her moment of amused sarcasm, then said, 'I'm used to being without modern conveniences, Peta. Every country, every situation, has its drawbacks as well as its benefits.'

'What made you want to go abroad in the first place?'

For a few moments Ashley seemed unable to reply. He ran his fingers round his empty cup deep in thought.

'Don't you ever feel the need to do something for no specific reason?' In the pale candleglow Peta could see that he had become solemn and wasn't expecting her to reply. 'I could sound noble and say that I felt called to go out there to work, but that wouldn't be true, only in as much as I recognised the horrors of malnutrition and starvation. I was appalled at the numbers of children dying in Ethiopia, for instance, so I made a snap decision.'

He fell silent and Peta asked, 'You feel it was the right decision? After all, we can't *all* go rushing off to trouble spots around the world at a moment's notice.'

'I thought it was the right decision at the time.'

'You wouldn't do it again?'

He looked up defensively. 'On the contrary,' he said adamantly, 'I'm only sorry I didn't go sooner, and I'll return in due course. It's a completely different life out there so one needs to return home occasionally, partly to catch up on the modern world, partly to rest, but most of all to freshen one's outlook on priorities.'

'But what about your family? Don't they figure in your priorities? Quentin seemed surprised you hadn't wanted to spend Christmas with your parents if you haven't seem them for a long time.'

'My priorities and Quentin's are totally different, my dear Peta. Although as twin brothers we have a lot in common, we also live entirely separate lives.' He stood up with a sudden movement, and at that moment the lights came on.

Ashley looked across at Peta, who was struggling to disentangle her feet from her dressing-gown, and smiled in a relaxed way. 'There,' he said, 'I should have stood up sooner. Now I don't need the candles, but you'd better keep them handy in case of a repeat. I'll be shopping tomorrow so I'll get some for myself.'

Peta managed to uncurl from the chair and Ashley took a step closer to her, stretching out a hand to feel her hair.

'It's still damp,' he said. 'Better finish your beauty treatment before you go to bed.' Although he smiled gently as he squeezed Peta's arm, she noticed that his dark-tanned features were creased with lines of strain.

He left the flat quickly after checking that all the candles were safely extinguished and Peta felt suddenly melancholy. He was a man with problems—personal ones, and she guessed she had added to his complications by asking about Africa. Or was it something to do with his parents and Tenerife which had brought about the change in him?

She poured herself more coffee. Fool, she reprimanded, now she'd never sleep, but she sat on her bean-bag on the floor in front of the fire drying her hair and styling it with a small brush while she visualised the kind of life Ashley had been living abroad.

He admitted to making a snap decision to go, so life in England must at that time have seemed empty. Was he bored? Was he perhaps escaping from family ties? He didn't really seem the type of man who would ever run from his commitments, so Peta decided that what he had said was true. He saw a country and its people in need of help and he simply offered himself. He was *that* dedicated.

No wonder he had high values and a set of standards which few could equal—certainly not her, she thought dismally. She could only admire his devotion to his work, but as she pondered over all that she was learning about her new tenant she felt convinced that underlying the passion for his chosen profession there was a man with some hidden bitterness. Not so hidden either, she reminded herself as she remembered his change of mood when in his brother's company.

Quentin was so easy to get on with. Quick-witted and with a ready charm to attract female attention. Ashley had remarked about his brother's outgoing character almost as if he were jealous of him. There was a barrier between them, she was sure. For one thing, Ashley's manner changed noticeably when Quentin was around. Could it be something to do with their parents, she wondered again? Or was it Tenerife? Who or what in Tenerife had urged Ashley to take up a new post only days before Christmas when, as Quentin had remarked, the Canary islands would have been the ideal spot to relax and help the acclimatisation process?

The twin brothers were about thirty-five years of age. Strange that neither of them had married, she mused.

Next morning she was up early, having slept reasonably well in spite of too much coffee. The wind had howled eerily round the house during the night, but it appeared to have had a soothing effect and now the first thing Peta did was to draw her curtains aside and peer out through the frost-patterned windows.

The children had broken up from school so the delivery of papers was being done in between snow-ball fights, and Peta wished she was young enough to go out there and join the paper boys and girls. Even if no more snow fell, it was going to be a white Christmas. Several inches covered the ground and it was still too cold for a thaw to set in. Better to have it now all in one spell, she thought, and this latest blizzard had confirmed that her decision not to go to Sussex had been the right one. She had a cosy flat, plenty to eat and drink, and all the festivities she'd need going on at Gida's. It wouldn't be quite the same though as being with family.

For a moment or two she allowed self-pity to overrule common sense. Then as she turned away from the window she told herself not to be so weak-minded. She wasn't the only person who would spend Christmas alone and there were many far less fortunate than her. At least the hospital atmosphere suited the occasion, and her task was to give the children of Angelique ward as good a time as was possible in the circumstances.

She wasn't due on duty until mid-morning so she had time to walk to a nearby parade of shops, but on the way she stopped off at Mrs Hubbard's house. She went round to the kitchen window and looked in and saw the elderly lady at the sink.

'Anything you need from the shops, Mrs Hubbard?' she called.

Mrs Hubbard motioned to Peta to come in, and a few seconds later opened the door with a struggle as the packed snow round the weatherboard crunched and finally gave way.

'I'll just stand inside,' Peta said. 'Mustn't let your heat escape, and there's the possibility I'll melt all over your floor. You are keeping warm and having plenty of soup and hot drinks?'

Mrs Hubbard was in her early eighties but a pleasant motherly sort who was fairly fit, and anxious to be left in her own home as long as she was able.

'Bless you, Peta, my dear, I shan't get cold nor

starve, and I don't mean to go visiting *this* Christmas.'

Peta laughed with the old lady. 'I'm afraid I shan't be home until late this evening, Mrs Hubbard, and I shall be at the hospital all over Christmas, but I'll try to look in and see you sometime. Here's my home telephone number and the hospital one in case you need me.'

'You are a good, kind girl, Peta, but don't worry none, I shall be warm and cosy with Snudge and my telly for company.'

'How about shopping? Are you sure you have everything you need?'

'Had a lovely hamper delivered to me yesterday. I know you haven't got time today, my dear, but when you come in again I'll show you. I shall never eat half of it so you can take what you like from it.'

'I'd love to see it, but I'm all slushy and snowy at the moment. It's yours, Mrs Hubbard, so you must use everything yourself. What are you having for your Christmas dinner?'

'Got a nice little capon for Snudgie and me. We shall be fine, Peta, but I shall look forward to you coming over for a cup of tea when you have a bit of off duty time. I want to hear all about the babies and those poor little mites who have to spend Christmas in bed. Oh yes, *and* I want to hear all about your new lodger.'

Mrs Hubbard dried her hands on a small kitchen towel and picked up the small tabby cat which rubbed around her legs.

'Not lodger, Mrs Hubbard,' Peta said. 'He's the tenant in the ground floor flat.' She sighed. 'I'm not at all sure that it's going to work, but I suppose I shall get used to having some strange person in the other half of the house.'

'He *looks* nice, and you'll feel more secure with a man about the place. Ivor knew what he was doing all right, and in spite of what you think about your brother, he does care about you.'

'He's got enough on his plate with his own family, but, yes, I suppose he cares in his own funny way.'

More about getting his half-share of the house, Peta thought, but she couldn't tell Mrs Hubbard that. Like so many elderly ladies she had a soft spot for boys who could twist her round their little finger.

'You just take care of your mum, Snudge,' Peta added, making a fuss of the cat before she left, and then she went on her way, trudging cautiously through the crisp snow and turning her thoughts to the hundred and one things she had to organise on Angelique ward.

On the corner of the High Street she passed the local greengrocer's shop and she waved and called a greeting to the two young brothers who ran the shop for their parents.

'Have a nice Christmas, and don't work too hard, Miss Blair,' Robert called. He was such a nice lad, not yet twenty but a real heart-stopper, not only because of his good looks but also because of his kind, friendly manner. 'Can I put some sprouts by for you?' he added. 'A bit pricey but they're nice ones.'

'And don't forget the mistletoe!' Steve, the younger and more cheeky of the two added. His reminder stopped Peta from walking on. She turned and slowly retraced her steps.

'Now, that I *had* forgotten,' she admitted. 'Not that it'll do me much good, but I'll have a few sprigs for the ward and my flat. I shan't need any sprouts though, Robert. I shall be eating at Gida's for much of the time and I've plenty of frozen veg if I'm home.'

Robert and Steve took down a huge bunch of mistletoe and instead of separating the twigs Robert pushed it into Peta's hand.

'If it's for the hospital have it on us, and even if it isn't, it's still yours as long as I can have the first kiss.'

Peta smiled, not easily, with the keen winds freezing her face, but both boys pecked her cheek which evoked a few honks from car horns and wolf whistles, and the butcher from the next shop held up a queue of customers to come and follow suit.

'I'm going before we stage a riot in the High Street,' Peta said, laughing merrily.

With much exchanging of good wishes she passed on down the road, suddenly aware of the growing festive spirit. Life, she thought, is what you make it. It was up to her to enjoy herself and stop feeling guilty about Ivor and his family. The family tie might prompt him to spare a thought for Peta but she wouldn't, or need not be lonely. Suddenly the anticipation of the children in the wards finding their jumbo-sized stockings filled with goodies gave her a tremendous feeling of happiness and she quickened her pace.

There were still two normal working days before Christmas Eve, and today Ossy would be round deciding who could go home and who would have to stay. As Peta carefully picked her way over the now muddy-looking snow on the main street, she felt torn in two ways. Marty Alexander was a special baby to his parents so it was right that he should go home, but Peta had really set her heart on keeping him for herself for Christmas.

She was being foolish, of course; over the years she had learnt not to become too attached to patients whatever their age. She managed a gentle smile. Maybe it was the maternal instinct making itself apparent at last. She'd got the home, all she needed was the man—but she'd got that too, she reminded herself drily. He was going to be around for quite a while, and he would be doing a round later today with her beloved Ossy.

Somehow Mr Ashley Reeves had intruded into her comfortable, steady way of life and spoilt its familiar pattern. But there was Quentin too, and she harboured a secret desire to see him again. That would surely brighten her Christmas.

It took her a little while to get used to the extreme heat inside the hospital. The rest of the staff were much amused by the amount of mistletoe she'd brought and gradually, as word spread around, the bunch diminished in size until only one generous sprig remained. She hid it in the linen cupboard, vowing her nurses to secrecy until she had time to put it up over the main doors.

Parents were in and out constantly, some a help, others a little too demanding in their nervous state at having children remain in hospital over Christmas.

Peta sat at her desk and read the night report,

noting with satisfaction that baby Marty Alexander had managed to keep most of his feeds down and had slept well in between them. She went on to familiarise herself with the more detailed account of the two young boys admitted yesterday, both suffering from compound fractures after a tobogan-ning tumble. As soon as she finished reading about the rest of the patients she went through to the boy's ward.

Neil and Simon were pale and subdued, and at the moment Peta greeted them were giving instruc-tions of their requirements to their anxious parents.

'A fine mess you two have got yourselves into for the holiday,' Peta said cheerfully. Neil's mother stood up, showing signs of the agitation her son's admission had caused.

'Sister, isn't there any chance of us having Neil home for Christmas?' she begged.

Peta shook her head. 'I'm afraid not. I'm sorry for you all, but they do need hospitalisation for a few days. You can come in and out as you please, of course, provided the boys have plenty of time to rest in between your visits.'

'I'll have my mother with us on Christmas Day, but we'll all come in for tea if that's all right.'

'Of course, and what about you, Mrs Bright?'

'I'm afraid I've got family for Christmas dinner but I'll come in for an hour about teatime, and you just try turning me away on Boxing Day. We'll have to have a second Christmas when Simon gets home.'

'That's right,' Peta agreed, 'and we'd better have some extra pyjamas for both boys. We do keep some for emergencies but I have a nasty feeling we might be needing them. Orthopaedics are already full to overflowing, and Casualty bears all the signs of turning into a refugee camp. It'll be a help if Neil and Simon have their own things.'

Peta did her best to reassure both patients and their parents. Apart from the compound fractures of arms and legs, both boys had an array of cuts and bruises on their faces and other parts of their bodies.

'You match our decorations,' she told them with a warm smile, and then she visited the rest of the children in her care.

The physiotherapist was having fun with Gary Llewellyn during his therapy in preparation for going home.

'He's going to make his mum's Christmas a very special one,' Peta said, smiling at the little boy. 'We're going to miss you, young man. In spite of how ill you've been, you've always had a smile for us.'

She moved on to the older children, Sarah-Jayne whose fingers had been wired in order to save the nails, and Stephanie, who seemed so frail and tearful.

She chatted to them for a while and then went to see Paul Newton who was being constantly special-led. His parents' presence was doing much to help him lie quietly, and according to all the reports it seemed likely that with bed-rest and careful nursing he had a chance of complete recovery.

The evening was closing in too early, Peta decided later when parents had left and the babies were all asleep in their cots. Only an occasional murmur of voices came from the boy's ward where a small television was on and a cowboy film holding the interest of those well enough to watch.

'It's really time you all settled down,' Peta said. 'How long does the film go on for?'

'It finishes at nine—oh, please, Blah, Blah,' one of the longer duration inmates pleaded. 'We usually have it on until you go home.'

'But there's Neil and Simon to consider now.'

It seemed, though, that for all their discomfort the new admissions were eager to see the film through, so Peta left them, supervised for a few minutes the preparation of stocking presents and then remembered her sprig of mistletoe.

It had lots of berries and she thought how generous Robert and Steve had been. Where should she put it? She doubted that the children would even notice so she decided on a spot above the double swing doors leading into the entrance passage of Angelique ward. It needed to go up high to clear the doors opening and closing, so she fetched a stool and fastened the mistletoe to the wall with a drawing pin, along with some streamers of red and gold ribbon.

Just as she was about to hold the door handle to get down she realised it wasn't there. Dr Mandeville was holding the door open, and behind him stood Ashley Reeves.

'So, Pet, we've arrived just in time, I see,' Dr Mandeville said as he spread his arms, inviting Peta to fall into them—which she did. And then the middle-aged consultant held her affectionately while he kissed her—probably more lingeringly than was necessary.

'I'll just go and peep at Paul Newton while you

enjoy your Christmas kiss, Ashley,' Ossy said then as he freed Peta.

In the poor lighting of the corridors it wasn't easy to see Ashley's features clearly. That he didn't speak or move towards her suggested his dislike of such familiarity. Peta straightened her apron and cap, and was about to mutter something to the effect that he need not copy the consultant's frivolous gesture when he suddenly took her by surprise, grasping her fiercely, drawing her backwards into his arms, then kissing her with an almost demented passion.

Peta's head began to reel and yet she was in no position to struggle in spite of beating against his shoulder with her free hand. Inwardly she was fighting for breath. Would he never release her!

CHAPTER FIVE

WHEN Ashley did free her she looked round in
agitation to see who was about while she panted
indignantly.

'It's all right, Peta, no one saw,' he whispered,
and hurried after the consultant. Peta followed,
knowing that if she waited until she was fully recovered she would feel more embarrassed than in
her present state of flushed dishevelment.

Fortunately there was hardly any light in Paul
Newton's room and he was sleeping peacefully, so
by the time Peta led the way to her office she had
managed to effect an outward calm.

'So, Pet, my dear, how are all the preparations
going?' Ossy asked, placing his arm round her
shoulder.

'Fairly well.' As she tried to form the words she
realised that her lips were swollen and she felt the
blood rush to her cheeks. Whatever did Ashley
Reeves think he was playing at? Trying to do better
than Ossy? Or show her that he could equal his
brother's style?

'I'm sorry that you didn't get the time off which I
feel you need,' Ossy was saying, 'but in these
circumstances Gida's need is greater than your
family's. At least I shall go away with an easy mind,
and you and Ashley will have a chance to get to
grips with the needs of our patients without any
interference from me.' He smiled reassuringly,

probably recognising the flicker of doubt which crossed Peta's face even as he was speaking.

'Now, my dear, I think we ought to decide who we can send home for Christmas. If this weather continues you're probably going to have your hands full with emergency admissions, plus the fact that for some of these youngsters, staying here won't help their progress. So they may just as well be in the comfort of their own homes. The parents will be spared difficult travelling conditions too, so let's see what we can do.'

Peta sat at her desk, not daring to glance at Ashley who thankfully had to take the chair farthest from her for the next forty minutes while each case was discussed thoroughly.

Quite a long list of children who were now well enough to convalesce at home eventually emerged. It was decided that the not so cut and dried cases such as Marty Alexander and Stephanie, who was really unhappy, could be sent home for Christmas with the proviso of an early appointment in the new year at Ashley's outpatient clinic.

When the two men had left Angelique ward Peta found herself with only half her mind on the remaining jobs to be done. The effect of Ashley's kiss had been disturbing, to say the least!

The most junior of the nurses came to her to report that the Christmas tree was now finally complete with crackers and chocolate animals hanging on it, as well as other small gifts.

Peta went to admire their handiwork and then sent them off duty a few minutes early as they were all going to the carols rehearsal.

Handing over to the night staff took longer than

usual while Peta explained about the discharges, and the next morning her first task was to telephone the parents so that they would come as early as possible to take their children home. It was a hectic day, with previous patients visiting the wards and bringing gifts to show their appreciation of past care.

A school choir arrived immediately after lunch, accompanying younger children who performed a moving nativity pageant, and this necessitated bringing the older boys into the main ward. Then followed some carol singing, which everyone participated in and thoroughly enjoyed.

Although there were fewer patients, already a bond was drawing them together in close harmony, and the older boys seemed to be quite happy to move to beds in one section of the main ward for the Christmas period. Only the few babies remained in their own ward, but they were moved to the top end where it joined the main ward so that they could see the Christmas tree lights.

While the school choir was singing, Peta went to spend some time with her smallest patients. She nursed each one as she sang softly along with the choir, and then moved into the main ward. Of those going home, most had already left. Some were ready, but their parents were keen to enjoy the concert before they went on their way.

Peta looked along the row of neat beds. In the dim lighting coming only from the Christmas tree, as the afternoon faded into evening, she noticed that Stephanie's parents hadn't yet arrived and that the little girl was lying on her side, the bedcovers pulled up to her chin.

Peta made her way silently to Stephanie's bed and as she peered down she realised that huge tears were tumbling from the child's eyes.

'Stephanie,' she whispered softly, 'it's all right, darling, you're going home today.'

Stephanie turned and flung her arms round Peta's neck.

'She . . . isn't coming, Sister . . . no one's coming for me,' she hiccuped.

Peta let her cry—loud, heart-rending sobs which brought a lump to the nurse's throat.

'Ssh,' she consoled as she gently rocked her to and fro. 'Of course Mummy's coming. I told you this morning that I'd spoken to her on the telephone.'

'Then why doesn't she come?'

'I expect it's this awful weather. Does Mummy drive?'

Stephanie nodded. 'She can, but Daddy won't let her much. He needs the car most.'

'I expect she's busy, anyway. There's always last minute shopping to do, and she may want to wait until your Daddy's home because you've got a younger brother and sister, haven't you?'

The sobs continued, gradually diminishing in sound, but Peta could feel the vibrations of the delicate little body against her own.

It was all so horribly unfair, so grossly unjust, she thought. No one had mentioned it yet, but a certain kind of gloom hung over Stephanie's bed because the very type of tests needed told the medical staff what was most feared. By instinct Peta felt certain that Stephanie had leukaemia, but no one would dare mention such a thing just before Christmas.

That chemotherapy treatment would be needed was almost a foregone conclusion, but Peta was concerned that this particular patient might not respond in the way most children did.

'Come on, Stephanie,' she suddenly encouraged brightly, 'let's get your dressing-gown on ready for when Mummy and Daddy arrive.'

'That's an excellent suggestion, Sister.'

Peta glanced over her shoulder to find Ashley just behind her.

'Have you enjoyed the concert, Stephanie?' he asked kindly, gently caressing Stephanie's cheek. She nodded and in a surprise move placed her other arm round Ashley's neck, drawing him into her circle.

'What's Father Christmas going to bring you?' Ashley asked with a broad smile.

'A nurse's uniform.' She gazed into Peta's face with fond admiration. 'I'm going to be a nurse when I grow up. Will I look as pretty as Sister Blair in my uniform?' she asked Ashley, her large, liquid eyes opening wider with enthusiasm.

'You'll be the prettiest nurse in the whole world,' he replied, hugging her affectionately.

'Not prettier than Sister Blair,' she said with a frown of doubt puckering her angelic face. 'My Daddy says he's never seen such a pretty nurse anywhere.'

'I'm sure your Daddy will agree with me that you'll be prettier even than Sister Blair.'

'Hey, you two,' Peta interrupted, struggling to chase away the lump that had seized her voice. 'Do you mind not discussing me!'

Stephanie was smiling now and, looking from

Ashley to Peta, she placed her pale cheek against Peta's face and said, 'I wish I could take you home with me.'

'Oh, come on,' Ashley responded with a mock hurt expression, 'and what will I do without her for Christmas?'

'You could come too,' she invited solemnly, and then her eyes lit up afresh as she caught sight of her parents coming into the ward.

The children and young people who had given the concert were now distributing presents to the patients.

'Come and see me in my office before you go, Mrs Holt,' Peta suggested. 'You can go to the bathroom to dress if you like, Stephanie.'

Ashley was already holding the door open and he followed Peta into her office.

'I forgot to mention earlier that a large parcel was standing against my patio doors when I went home at lunch-time. It's for you, so I took it in.'

'Oh, thanks. I must tell the postman. It's an arrangement we've always had that he leaves parcels there, not that I get that many.'

'No need to alter your arrangements. How long before you're off duty?'

'I should be off now. I came in fairly early today, but I'm not really keeping to any schedule over the holidays. I'm spare really, you see. As I should have been away, to save messing up the rota I'm sort of doing a nine to five shift, although I shall most likely still be here in the evenings to join in whatever there is to join in.' She was prattling on needlessly, trying not to look at him; trying to forget his powerful kiss.

'You're obviously not going to use your car in this weather so let me know if you want a lift any time. I've had chains fitted to the rear wheels of mine, so unless it's quite impossible to drive at all we shouldn't get stuck anywhere. How soon will you be ready now?'

'About half an hour, I should think. I must see the school children off, and Stephanie too.'

'Mm . . . Stephanie. She's very sweet. I wish—' he raised his arms in a negative gesture. 'But, we mustn't get depressed over Christmas. I'm going back to my office now to put together all our findings, but I don't need to tell you how it all adds up. Still, we must do our best for her. Give me a ring when you're ready, Peta, and I'll take you home.'

Peta thanked him and he left quickly, obviously preferring not to be asked too many awkward questions by Stephanie's parents at this early stage. Stephanie went off happily after presenting Peta with a gaily-wrapped gift for the nursing staff, and promising that she would call to see them all in Angelique ward when she visited Outpatients in the new year.

Peta managed to keep cheerful for the sake of the other children, even though she knew she would be seeing a lot more of Stephanie in the coming months.

There was a hum of expectancy everywhere at Gida's next day, and Peta managed not to dwell on the conversation she had shared with Ashley on the way home the previous evening. His diagnosis was conclusive, there was no point in trying to hide it, and a despondency had settled on both of them so that, on reaching fifty-six Vandyke Crescent, Ashley had handed over the huge parcel from Ivor and they had both retreated to their own flats. A large number of cards and letters were also awaiting Peta, which helped to halt her growing melancholy over Stephanie. Now, as she greeted the excited children, her resolve was to give her all to them, while children like Marty Alexander and Stephanie were in the security of their parents' love and attention.

She had been reluctant to part with Marty but his parents had looked overjoyed as they had carried him away, along with the teddy bear which Peta had selected for him. Seeing the happiness on the young couple's faces was well worth all the effort, and she just prayed that if she never saw Marty again it meant that he was well, and that surgery wouldn't be needed.

All morning was taken up with the administration of medication and dressings, particularly those of Neil and Simon, who today had more colour and had recovered from the initial shock of being admitted to hospital. At least they would feel more like taking part in the Christmas festivities now, and throughout the day there were numerous callers, including the Salvation Army band, songsters and young people with their tambourines, who gave great delight to the children on Angelique ward.

Snow fell heavily for most of the day and it was beginning to lose its appeal for everyone except the children. Hospital corridors were slushy and the staff in the Casualty department rushed off their feet, so when the night staff came on duty Peta offered her services in that department for the evening until it was time to tour the wards singing carols.

Fortunately many cases were nothing more than surface wounds and severe bruising, though there were several fractures to be set in plaster, and it was very late when a small child was rushed in by ambulance.

'One for you, Peta,' one of the young doctors called. 'A pre-Christmas binge on what the child thought were Smarties—her mum's pills, needless to say.'

Peta took the two-year-old girl to the treatment room and proceeded immediately with the necessary stomach washout, after which she took the child to be admitted to Angelique ward, accompanied by frightened parents.

'We'll have to keep her for forty-eight hours observation,' Peta explained. Then as Nicky, the Night Sister, took little Emma Brooks away into the babies' ward she placed a comforting hand on the distressed mother's arm. 'She'll be all right, don't worry. It just means you'll have to postpone Christmas for a couple of days.'

By the time Peta and Nicky had put the parents' minds at rest and Emma was settled in a cot sleeping soundly, Peta realised that the carol singing would be well under way. She turned her cloak inside out so that the red lining was uppermost and, with a slow-burning candle inside a small chromium lantern which had been a present from her parents at her first Christmas in training, she hurried through the corridors following the sound of music.

There was an atmosphere in hospital at Christmas-time. Something emotional, something indefinable, which caught at the heart of every doctor and nurse as well as the unfortunate patients.

Gida's boasted proudly of a fine choir, which now led the singing accompanied by various instrumentalists, guitarists, recorders and flautist.

They were singing 'Hark the Herald Angels Sing' as Peta caught up with the group in the maternity wing, and as they proceeded along the corridors a rich baritone voice joined in behind her. At the end of that carol and before the beginning of the next one, Ashley took Peta's lantern from her.

'Can I share your candle?' he whispered.

'Again?' Peta whispered back, feeling kindly disposed to everyone, even Ashley Reeves.

She turned the pages of the carol sheet while Ashley held the candle-lantern over it, and they walked together at the end of the procession which gradually made its way to the great hall at Gida's where, at midnight, the hospital chaplain conducted a short service.

Afterwards, warm punch and hot mince pies were served by the catering staff and the excitement of Christmas really began. There were plenty of festive kisses, with or without mistletoe, but wherever Peta moved, Ashley was not far behind. He seemed a different person, less austere and pleased to be introduced to many of Gida's staff who were friends of Peta.

Margaret Astley-Brown moved among her staff with good wishes, and when she came to Ashley she said, 'This is your first Christmas in England for some considerable time, I believe?'

'About four years,' he replied with a smile. 'I'd forgotten about hospital Christmases, but I think I'm going to enjoy this one.' He suddenly placed his arm around Peta and drew her against his shoulder. 'Peta has very kindly taken me under her wing.'

'That's good,' Margaret said, trying to ignore Peta's raised eyebrows. 'She'll be glad of some company, having to stay at home after all.'

Peta rather wished she hadn't said that, but it was Christmas, so she must be congenial.

When the Chief Nursing Officer said good night it was an indication that it was time for everyone to disperse.

'Meet me by the main entrance when you're ready,' Ashley said quietly. 'I'll fetch my coat and bring the car round.'

Peta returned to Angelique ward to change into her fur-lined boots, thick coat and woolly hat and mitts once more. She was a trifle envious of Nicky Terry.

'It must be fun playing Father Christmas,' she said, 'and really rewarding to see the expressions on the children's faces in the morning. The best of it will be over by the time I get here.'

'Probably the middle of the night,' Nicky said drily. 'I bet we don't get all the stockings round before someone wakes. Of course, you can always stay if you want to.'

'I'd better get a couple of hours sleep, I think,' Peta said, laughing at her friend's suggestion.

'How are you getting home, taxi?'

'No, Ashley Reeves is giving me a lift.'

'He's still here!'

'Yes, joined in the carol singing too.'

'I see!' Nicky said with a knowing smile. 'Stayed for that with an ulterior motive, I bet.'

'Oh, Nicky! You don't really think he did? No, he just wanted to be part of all that's going on.'

'Hurry up and don't keep him waiting,' Nicky urged. 'Lucky you, having an escort right on your doorstep.'

Peta wasn't sure that she was so lucky, especially if everyone was going to make innuendos about their relationship. She was grateful though, not to have to trudge through the snow storm which was in full force when she went outside. The journey home was a slow and precarious one.

'What time do you want to go back to Gida's? I'd better take you,' Ashley said before they parted.

'I'd like to go in early, but I can walk. I expect you have plans other than visiting the hospital.'

Ashley shook his head. 'I'm looking forward to meeting Mrs Mandeville. They invited me to join their party for Christmas lunch at the Galaxy Restaurant but I declined. I shall stay at Gida's for a while, then come home. Shall we say nine o'clock?'

Peta couldn't think of any excuses not to accept his kind offer, even though she was certain that he hadn't intended to go in that early, but by the time she was ready on Christmas morning after only five hours sleep, Ashley was already warming the car up. He held the door open for her to get in.

'Happy Christmas, Peta,' he said and stopped her to kiss her forcefully on the mouth.

'There's no mistletoe here,' she said with irritation, wondering how many prying eyes had witnessed the action from behind net curtains.

'You seemed to be doing well enough without it

last evening, and I'm sure your neighbours all thrive on a little gossip.'

'I try never to give them cause to gossip about me,' she said adamantly, 'that's why—' She halted.

'That's why you don't really approve of me as your tenant,' Ashley stated positively. 'I didn't think our generation worried about what people say any more. I'm pleased to know that my landlady guards her reputation so avidly, but I don't think you need worry, my dear Peta. Everyone will be too busy with their own affairs this morning.'

Except people like Mrs Hubbard, Peta thought. She wouldn't miss anything and she'd be ready to say so when Peta visited the old lady later on. It wasn't that she'd be unpleasant about it; she'd jump to conclusions and come up with the wrong answer, and in her excitement all Vandyke Crescent would be anxiously awaiting a wedding!

Ashley had cleared the frost on the windscreen once but it was settling again already. The snow clouds had gone at last, giving way to a clear, bright, sunny morning even though the temperatures were well below freezing. The snow crunched beneath the tyres, but with the aid of the chains on the rear wheels they were able to drive along the deserted streets to the hospital, and Peta was glad to get inside in the warm.

'I'll see you later on,' Ashley said and strode off towards the consultants' sitting-room.

Although there was more noise than usual coming from the wards, Peta had to sit down at her desk, read the night report and discuss a few minor points with Cathy.

The parents of little Emma Brooks had obviously

slept for only a very short time before anxiously returning to Gida's.

'We've brought her nightie, a brush and comb, dressing-gown and slippers,' Mrs Brooks said, still looking intensely pale as she leaned over Emma's cot.

'You can't have been to bed,' Peta said, 'but I understand Emma slept right through until you arrived. I think it would be a good idea if you were to bath her yourself, Mrs Brooks. She'll feel fresher and then she can run around in her dressing-gown if she wants to.'

'You've all been so kind,' Mrs Brooks said. 'All these presents—we didn't expect Father Christmas to know where to find you, did we, Emma?'

Peta spent a few minutes chatting to Emma and playing with the toys she had received, and then she went right through the ward, accepting a challenge from eleven year old Neil to a game of chess later on, as he had received a chess-set in his Christmas stocking.

There was a happy atmosphere with parents and relatives visiting and making the day as joyful as possible, and mid-morning Dr and Mrs Mandeville arrived while Peta was on the floor playing skittles with Emma Brooks.

'Merry Christmas, my dear,' Ossy said, helping Peta to her feet. Then Peta's gaze fell on Mrs Mandeville.

'Merry Christmas to both of you,' Peta said quickly, feeling the blood drain from her face, 'and a very happy holiday.'

Mrs Mandeville kissed Peta lightly and gave her a brightly-wrapped and beribboned gift.

Peta kept repeating her thanks awkwardly, not because she felt embarrassed at accepting their gift but because she was stunned at the sight of Mrs Mandeville. She appeared to have aged twenty years in only a few months, and Peta's first reaction was to question the sense in going away on holiday. To the Swiss Alps she remembered too, not the West Indies or somewhere where the warmth of the sun might do the sick woman some good.

'I love Switzerland,' Mrs Mandeville enthused, 'even though skiing is out for me this time.'

'You could have stayed home to do that this year,' Peta said, at last managing a smile.

'Ossy needs a holiday, Peta. It does him more good to get right away from Gida's and all the pressures for a couple of weeks. Of course, he'll be happiest when we're on the return flight,' she said, glancing at her husband.

Dr Mandeville inclined his head and exchanged the kind of understanding look with his wife which can only be shared by two people who are very close.

'Who wouldn't be, with the loveliest of nursing sisters to come home to?' he said, smiling at Peta.

Dr Mandeville then turned his attention to the children, while Mrs Mandeville went to the office with Peta for a small sherry.

They chatted for a few moments about the fact that Peta's holiday plans had of necessity been cancelled, and then Mrs Mandeville asked, 'And what do you make of Ashley Reeves?'

'Have you met him yet?' Peta countered.

'Just—a few moments ago. What a handsome

young man he is! Ossy tells me he's a fine paediatrician too, and he's unattached, Peta. We'll have you both to dinner when we get back.'

'No match-making, Mrs Mandeville,' Peta laughed, a trifle embarrassed at the way the colour flushed her cheeks to dark crimson.

'I don't need to, my dear. He's your tenant I understand, so you'll get to know one another very quickly, I'm sure.'

Peta had to keep her opinion to herself as Ossy evidently thought so highly of Ashley, but she wished she could share her thoughts with someone else because the very thing she had tried to prevent happening was in danger of shattering her daily routine. She couldn't deny that it was nice to have someone to take her to and from work in view of the dreadful weather conditions, but there was the fear that he would become too familiar, take her for granted, and she him, and their lives would become inseparable. Peta was determined to remain as independent as she had shown her brother Ivor she could be.

Her heart missed a beat. What were they all doing without her at this minute, she wondered? If she had gone to Sussex she would have been part of a real family Christmas. Perhaps she was taking this independence thing too seriously.

'Ah, there you are, my dear,' Ossy said to his wife, appearing in the doorway. 'Do you feel up to meeting the children now?'

Mrs Mandeville finished her drink and stood up, and no sooner had they gone into the ward than the telephone rang.

'Happy Christmas, Peta.'

'Happy Christmas, Ivor,' Peta's voice cracked emotionally. 'How nice of you to ring.'

Somehow she couldn't control or stem the flow of tears which trickled annoyingly down her cheeks, but she bravely forced her voice to speak happily. And indeed she was happy that Ivor and Ros had thought of her on this Christmas morning.

She was blowing her nose vigorously and wiping away a persistent tear after she had put the phone down, when Ashley and Quentin appeared in the doorway.

CHAPTER SIX

'PETA, is something wrong?' Ashley asked with genuine concern.

'No, of course not. I think I'm going to have a cold,' she said, wishing desperately that these two men hadn't chosen to arrive at that moment.

'I hope you don't mind but I've brought Quentin to meet our patients and do the rounds with me. I believe it's the consultant's job to carve the turkey in the ward?'

'That's right,' Peta said, giving a last little sniff but able to face the two brothers now.

'Thank goodness Dr Mandeville's still here then—I'm pretty hopeless at carving,' Ashley said.

'I should have thought you had just the right delicate touch for such a job,' Quentin said with a grin.

'Perhaps *too* delicate,' Ashley retorted.

'What time's lunch?' Quentin pretended to ignore his brother.

'About twelve, so that the consultants can all go home to their own parties, and there'll be two sittings in the canteen for the staff's Christmas dinner if you're staying,' Peta explained.

'Yes, we're staying. What time will you be going to have yours?' Ashley asked.

'I shall go second sitting. It's more fun for the junior nurses to go for the main sitting. It's usual for the sisters to go to the later one on Christmas Day.'

'We'll see you in the canteen then,' Ashley said.

'Please don't wait for me,' Peta said quickly. 'Most of your colleagues will be at the earlier one.'

'You aren't giving us the brush-off, I hope?' Quentin put in quickly. 'When I've travelled all this way just to see you?'

For a moment Peta allowed herself to be taken in by Quentin's flattery, but then she merely laughed it off and a few minutes later, when another consultant and his family came to visit Angelique ward, Dr and Mrs Mandeville left to go on to the maternity wing with Ashley and Quentin.

Most of the visiting parents stayed for a couple of hours and had gone home by the time dinner was served to the children. Dr Mandeville, complete with a high chef's hat, carved the turkey with great aplomb much to everyone's amusement, and Ashley helped Peta serve the vegetables.

The children hardly had time to realise that their parents had gone home, and after so much excitement were pleased to settle down quietly for the afternoon with their new toys and books.

Peta ensured that her young patients were comfortable while the rest of the staff went to the canteen. She busied herself tidying lockers and spent a few minutes with each child so that the ward was soon peaceful.

As was the usual custom at Gida's, one small room on each ward was gaily decorated and put at the disposal of the staff to entertain colleagues from other wards and any visiting VIPs. There were drinks, chocolates, nuts and various other goodies to be had and this was where Ashley and Quentin enjoyed an aperitif while waiting to escort Peta to the canteen.

'Have you time for a sherry?' Ashley asked her.

'No, thanks. It'll go to my head if I've had nothing to eat. If there's any left I'll have one afterwards.'

'Are you expecting your staff to hold an orgy while you're gone?' Quentin asked, laughing.

'No, though it's not unknown for some people to overdo it.'

She remembered Craig Murray and his invitation to a party in the resident doctor's lounge. There would be a discotheque during the evening so Peta looked forward to having a good time then, but right now she felt slightly embarrassed at having to go to the canteen with the two brothers.

Fancy hats were the order of the day and Peta wore a light blue one with a wide brim turned up on one side, decorated with silver and with a large ostrich feather curling up from the back.

The dining-room was almost full to capacity, even for the second sitting. Some of her colleagues had reserved a seat for Peta and as soon as they saw Ashley and Quentin they moved up, changed places and made quite a commotion in fact, so that Peta could sit between the two brothers.

She wished she had the courage to stand on her chair and announce that Ashley and his brother had chosen to wait for her, that it was no ploy on her part to encourage their attention, but by the many pairs of observant eyes focused on her she knew she was the envy of them all. Ashley was handsome, unmarried and in a prominent position at Gida's, which meant that there was no shortage of admiring females. The sooner one of them won him over the sooner he'd move out of the flat, she supposed, and wasn't that what she wanted?

She experienced a peculiar quiver of dismay at such a thought, but it was quickly forgotten as the party spirit developed rapidly with the splendid Christmas dinner, and Peta soon shed any embarrassment and joined in the merry-making with her colleagues.

Ashley was in conversation with the sister from the Outpatients department who was sitting next to him, and when coffee was served Quentin leaned closer to Peta.

'I rather hoped you would have been free today,' he whispered in her ear.

Peta felt the blood rush to her cheeks with excitement.

'I thought you came to spend Christmas with your brother,' she answered in a low voice.

'I turned down a few invitations, feeling that it was my duty to see that he wasn't spending the day alone, but there was an ulterior motive too.'

'I . . . I am free, but there's so much happening here, and I like being with the children,' she said, looking directly at him.

He didn't answer at once but gazed into her eyes, then his glance raked over her hat.

'You look slightly ridiculous in that pantomime creation,' he said, 'and I feel equally ridiculous in this pirate's hat.'

'We all look ridiculous together,' Peta consoled. 'Christmas doesn't last long, so we may as well make the most of it.'

'The sooner it's all over the better pleased I shall be,' Quentin said.

Peta turned on him with a look of protest, but he was grinning wickedly. 'Then I can take you out to dinner,' he added.

'When you're sober you'll regret making that suggestion,' she quipped, hoping that he meant it but not daring to believe him.

'I'm quite sober, Peta, and I mean it. I like parties but I'd prefer to be able to take you somewhere where we could be alone.'

With a pleading look she managed to silence him. Even with the babble of spirited voices around them she was convinced that somewhere a keen ear would catch the drift of the conversation.

'Better have your diary at the ready when I bring my men in to take down the decorations,' he said meaningfully. 'It looks as if I'm going to have to exercise patience.'

The catering staff were beginning to clear the tables and several people had already begun to leave, so Peta pushed back her chair. She didn't really think for one minute that Quentin had had too much to drink but she found his persistence disconcerting in such circumstances.

'I must get back to the ward,' she said. 'It must be nearly teatime for the children.'

Ashley turned aside from the other sister. 'Are we moving?' he asked, rising from his chair.

'You don't have to, but I must,' Peta said. 'Please stay.'

Quentin stood up, but Ashley gave her a quick nod and a slow smile before sitting down and eagerly resuming his conversation with Tracey Griffiths.

Peta hurried away, not daring to meet Quentin's searching gaze again, and her legs felt strangely wooden as she walked through the long corridors to Angelique ward. She had wanted Quentin to make a date, yet the fact that Ashley was there prevented her from being positive in her response. She supposed it was because she knew Ashley expected his brother not to waste any time in wooing her—but what did it matter to Ashley anyway, especially in the light of the growing friendship he had with Tracey? Now Peta reproached herself severely. That smacked of envy, and that was one thing she couldn't be when she was constantly seeking to find reasons for not having him in the other half of her house.

Tracey Griffiths was older than Peta by about five years. She was a tall, well built girl with plain features framed by black shiny curls and small dark eyes, which gave her a classic kind of appeal. She had no special friends yet was easy to get on with, and generally liked by everyone.

Peta found herself speculating about Tracey and Ashley. She would have assisted him in his frequent clinics, so by now they would be well acquainted. She couldn't imagine why the mental picture should aggravate her but it kept recurring as if to taunt her. Perhaps they might even be well suited, she thought idly as she slipped off her cuffs and rolled up her sleeves. But even that idea did nothing to appease the growing irritation.

Some of the nursing staff visiting from theatre and Outpatients helped with the children's tea and afterwards the youngest patients were washed and settled for the night while the older boys were allowed to watch television.

As Peta wrote her shorter than usual report she felt a chill despondency creeping over her. She had lost all enthusiasm for further festive celebrations and decided that it must be the effects of the wine, so she decided to go off duty as soon as Nicky reported. The walk home would clear her head and then she could please herself how she spent the rest of the evening. But Cathy wouldn't hear of it.

'Craig's expecting us to at least show our faces in the doctors' lounge,' she said. 'Dad's coming to pick me up about ten o'clock so he'll run you home, Peta.'

'But that's out of your way and I wouldn't like to keep you from your family gathering.'

'You could come back home with us—better than going to your own flat alone,' Cathy suggested kindly.

In the end Peta agreed to stay on for the party for a short while. Already there was some too-loud music blaring forth and groups of men and girls chatting and giggling.

Craig placed an arm around Peta and Cathy.

'I came for my Christmas kiss,' he said to Peta, 'but you were disappearing down the corridor with two men.'

He poured drinks for both girls and then guided Peta to a corner of the room where he kissed her very forcefully.

'You've had too much to drink,' Peta told him, pushing him away.

'So? It's Christmas and I'm over five hundred

miles away from home, Peta. Come on, let's dance.'

He pulled her towards him and still holding their drinks they gyrated in rhythm to the music. Craig was a lively, vigorous man, full of good humour and energy, so that Peta was soon drawn out of her earlier despondency.

When their drinks were finished Craig took away the empty glasses and returned to take Peta in his arms, guiding her slowly round the room. She felt quite tired and yet in a hazy way wondered why she hadn't brought a dress to change into for the evening. It didn't seem right to be dancing in her uniform. She would soon go home, she decided, but wearily rested her head on Craig's shoulder.

'What a pity I'm going home to Ayr for New Year,' Craig whispered. 'I think I fancy spending it with you.'

Peta glanced up at him with a smile, but a smile which quickly faded when, over Craig's shoulder, she saw Ashley standing by the door watching her. Then he left the room, closing the door behind him, and it wasn't until several minutes later that Peta's mind cleared sufficiently for her to realise that he had probably been trying to indicate that he was ready to leave.

So, she'd have to walk, and that would do her good, she thought positively.

'I think I shall have to go,' she said to Craig a little while later.

'I'm not in a fit state to drive you home, Pet,' Craig said.

'I think I'll walk—thanks for the party.'

Suddenly she wanted to get away. Ashley's critical look had dissolved her party spirit to a feeling of guilt, and yet she had no reason to feel guilty. She was entitled to enjoy herself, which she had been doing with her colleagues—a perfectly normal way to spend Christmas. Why should one withering glance from him affect her so utterly?

Peta searched and found Cathy, as usual chatting to other nurses rather than dancing.

'See you tomorrow, Cathy,' Peta said. 'I'm going now.'

'Dad wouldn't mind taking you home, honestly,' Cathy persisted, but Peta remained adamant. She went back to Angelique ward and dressed up in her warm clothes ready to face the cold night air.

'It's freezing out,' Nicky said, 'so mind you don't slip on the ice. We don't want you admitted and off work for weeks.'

'I'll try not to,' Peta said.

When she reached the main entrance she paused as the wind whistled round her legs and instantly stung her cheeks. It was a different world outside the warmth of Gida's—a very white one. She pulled her scarf up round her chin, tugged at her woolly hat and set off, her feet crunching on the snow.

She had walked the length of the driveway, past the ornamental tubs of shooting bulbs, now protected by their white coverlet of snow, and was approaching the edge of the car park when something thudded in the centre of her back. She spun round and the second snowball hit her shoulder, a third her forehead. She shrieked and held her arms up to shield her face, but they still kept coming rapidly.

When she heard the deep-toned laughter she

knew who her assailant was. By the speed and persistence of the snowballs she thought Quentin must be there too, so she flung down her bag and began to retaliate when she realised it was Ashley on his own. It was a fair fight and she was determined to hold her own, albeit briefly as, after aiming at his face and hitting him, her target began to give chase.

They dodged in and out of the cars but finally Peta found herself cornered. Ashley came towards her slowly while she panted for breath. She knew he had a handful of snow so she hid her face behind her soggy, wet gloves.

'Where would you like it?' he asked in a low seductive voice. 'Inside or out?'

'Neither,' she pleaded breathlessly.

He held her tightly with one arm and, lifting her skirts, pushed the snow into the top of her knee-high boots.

'You're rotten,' she cried struggling, but the nearness of him, the warmth of his breath on her tingling cheeks, the firmness of his hold made her relax. He was looking directly into her face, his expression soft, and she yielded spontaneously. His mouth came down on hers with a crushing impact, and soon she was glowing from her feet up.

'I would be a rotten swine,' he whispered, 'if I'd left my landlady to walk home. I considered a little healthy exercise was what you needed, my girl, and now I'll drive you home and you can get into some dry clothes.'

'It's you who've made them wet,' she responded petulantly.

'So? You're never too old to enjoy a snowball

fight. Tomorrow I'll make you a giant snowman.'

'I'm hardly ever at home to see it,' she said, 'but the children in hospital would love you to make them one.'

He pursed his lips thoughtfully and she expected him to find an excuse for not agreeing, but he placed his arm around her shoulder and guided her to his car.

'On condition that you come back and have some supper with me.'

Peta hesitated, and Ashley took the opportunity of kissing her again, a long, lingering kiss that flooded her veins with a new kind of sparkling exhilaration.

'Has Quentin gone on ahead?' she asked.

Ashley let her go. Peta felt his irritation as he unlocked the passenger door for her.

'Quentin has gone back to base. You'll have to make do with me, I'm afraid,' he said shortly.

He drove back to Vandyke Crescent in a rather reckless manner. Peta tried to think up words to explain her question, which had been asked in all innocence and not from desire to see Quentin at that particular moment. She genuinely had just recalled that he had come to Gida's to spend the day with Ashley, so it was a natural conclusion that he would end the evening at his brother's flat.

'I . . . I thought perhaps he was spending the night at your flat,' she offered in an endeavour to make amends. 'I presume he doesn't have to work over Christmas?'

'I understand there are some duties he has to attend to tomorrow. He *said* he came to spend today with *me*, but when he saw you dancing with

Craig so intimately he remembered his own friends at Plymouth, and he left in a hurry.'

'Is that *my* fault?' Peta asked crossly.

Ashley drew up at the wrought iron gates and then he looked across at Peta with a provocative smile.

'No—not directly, I suppose. In fact, if his leaving was on your account you've done me a favour. I can live comfortably without my brother's company.' His smile broadened. 'Now be a pet and open the gates for me—please?'

She got out of the car and let out an impatient sigh. Somewhere along the line she had lost out to him, but what was the contest all about, if indeed there was a contest at all?

By the time Ashley had put the Granada in the garage and closed the door, Peta was securing the latch on the outside gates. She stood for a moment looking across the road. It was too late to visit Mrs Hubbard now, even though a light still burned in the downstairs front room she used as a bedroom. A few doors farther on Mr Collins' house was in darkness. He'd have retired early as his son and family were coming down from Bath tomorrow to take him back there until after New Year.

Ashley unlocked his front door as Peta fitted her key in the lock.

'It's only just after ten,' Ashley said in a sober voice, 'I thought we might as well share some supper, a drink and watch television. But if you're tired . . . ?'

'No, no,' she half laughed. 'I was just thinking about poor old Mrs Hubbard who's only had her Snudge for company. If the weather had been better and I'd been driving, I would have popped back during the early evening to spend a few minutes with her.'

'You'd like to go now? I'll come too, so that you can introduce us,' he suggested eagerly.

'No, it's too late. Her bedroom light is on and I don't want to alarm her. I did pop over last evening for an hour. She likes to chat. She's got my telephone number here and at Gida's if she needs me.'

'You'd best get out of those wet boots.' He pulled off her woolly hat and pushed it against her cheek playfully. 'If you're going to start worrying about your neighbours I shall be tempted to roll you in the snow and that will surely bring out an audience.' He gave her a friendly push inside. 'I'll see you in ten minutes. Come straight in.'

Peta felt refreshed after a quick wash and replacement of her light make-up. She changed into a pink knitted dress which showed off her slim figure, accentuating her curves, and high-heeled navy blue patent court shoes.

She wondered, as she went down the stairs, what supper was going to consist of and whether it would have been courteous to take some of her pastries down with her. But they were all solidly frozen. She hadn't anticipated needing anything from her freezer for a couple of days while she was spending so much time at Gida's.

'Is there anything you need, Ashley?' she asked as she closed his front door firmly.

'Only you,' he joked. 'Come along in and get warm. I haven't caused you to get frostbite, have I?'

'Not from a few snowballs. Can I do anything?'

'No, darling—just do justice to my humble efforts.'

She preceded him into the lounge where the gas fire glowed vigorously and the illuminated log effect added some festive cheer to the room.

She suppressed a gasp when she noticed a small gateleg table opened and set for two with a Christmassy table-cloth and napkins, and the centrepiece made up of driftwood, leaves, red and gold baubles and three lighted candles standing in the midst of some holly. It looked most effective, especially when Ashley came in with bowls of steaming hot soup and turned off the centre and wall lights.

'You can't have prepared all this since you came home,' she said in surprise.

'When Quentin left I came back here for an hour, then returned to Gida's to fetch you. As far as the food goes, I only had to warm the soup, and the mince pies are in the oven.'

'But . . .' Peta stopped. How could she tell him that she didn't need or want him to fuss over her? It would have been ungracious when he had evidently gone to so much trouble to impress her.

'How did I know you'd accept my invitation?' He answered her thoughts. 'You had to come home tired and hungry eventually.' He pulled out a chair and when she was seated at the table he poured her a glass of white wine. Then from the other side of the table he raised his glass to her.

'To you from me, Peta, with my sincere thanks for having me here at Vandyke Crescent.'

She appreciated his thoughtfulness and a moment later lifted her glass to him. 'Here's to your stay here, and a long and happy appointment at Gida's.'

'You're very kind, my dear,' he said slowly, then hesitating briefly added, 'but not a long appointment. There's a greater need in Africa than here. A need for doctors and nurses alike; well-qualified people, dedicated medical staff who are willing to work in sometimes dangerous and primitive surroundings in outlying villages. The time I spend at Gida's is to act as a refresher course in new drugs and methods.'

'You intend to dedicate the rest of your life to working in darkest Africa?' she asked, her soup spoon suspended midway to her lips.

'Why not? What is there to keep me in England?'

Peta shrugged. 'I . . . I don't know. But wouldn't you like to be married for instance, and have children of your own?'

She saw a frown crease his brow, then he placed his spoon in his soup bowl and stared across at her with an intensity which was frightening. The candles flickered, casting eery shadows across his lean face, already shades paler than when he had first arrived.

'Yes, Peta,' he admitted. 'I'd love to be married and have at least six children, but my wife will have to be a very special kind of woman. She too must be dedicated to the work I'm involved in.'

'Isn't that asking rather a lot of any woman?' Peta asked. 'Couldn't you have your children first? I mean, I think most English girls would prefer to have their babies delivered by English midwives and doctors, and in an English hospital.'

'Always supposing I marry an English girl,' Ashley said pompously.

Peta finished her soup. Was this going to be another argument or a friendly discussion? Ashley took away the empty soup bowls and returned with a green salad to go with a salmon dish he had prepared himself.

'Something fairly light, I thought, after our rather filling Christmas dinner,' he explained. 'One tends to eat more when the weather is so cold.'

They ate in comparative silence for a while.

'So you think I'm destined to remain a bachelor if I'm determined to return to Africa?' he pursued.

'I didn't say that,' she answered quickly. 'I'm sure there are qualified nurses who would like to go abroad and live in a hot climate.'

'There are female doctors too, Peta, but why anyone in the medical profession? Unless, of course, you're suggesting . . . thinking . . . offering?' he arched an eyebrow quizzically.

'No!' Now he was getting her all confused. Who had started this silly conversation anyway? He could marry the Queen of Sheba for all she cared!

She knew he was gently making fun of her and because it was Christmas she reacted in a frivolous way, but lurking in the back of her mind she remembered a conversation she'd had with Nicky quite recently. A few years ago she'd had plenty of spirit and given the right opportunity would have willingly gone anywhere in order to gain valuable experience as well as seeing something of the world.

'Perhaps,' Ashley said, 'I am expecting a lot of the woman I shall marry. Her love will have to be everlasting, enduring . . .' He stared into the flames of the candles. 'Not like the candles,' he continued thoughtfully, 'burning slowly away, giving light and pleasure for only a short time. It will have to be a lifetime's faithfulness—am I being selfish, Peta? Am I expecting too much of any woman?'

'That must surely depend on the woman,' Peta replied.

CHAPTER SEVEN

So THAT was it, Peta thought, when he went to fetch the mince pies and make the coffee, refusing to allow her to help in any way. There was a woman, perhaps one who was not prepared to go to the far corners of the earth, even for the man she loved. It made her go cold inside. She almost felt sorry for Ashley. She tried to feel some sympathy for the unknown woman. Now she knew the reason that he had come back to England for a time, and such thoughts oddly disturbed her.

After the coffee and mince pies, and when the wine bottle was empty, Peta insisted on washing up. And suddenly the direction of the conversation changed. Ashley wanted to know about her family and how she had spent Christmases in the past, and inevitably Gida's hospital was soon the main topic again.

'I expect you know about Ossy's wife?' Peta said as she dried her hands.

'He told me himself,' Ashley replied solemnly.

'She looked so aged today, so vastly changed I could hardly believe it, much less that he could think of taking her to the Swiss Alps.'

'But if that is the kind of holiday she likes,' Ashley began, but Peta cut him short.

'She was always a vivacious, active woman. Very modern and sophisticated, but in her condition now surely they should have stayed at home?'

'I imagine Dr Mandeville would give her just about anything to make her last days happy ones, Peta. Who are we to judge what other people do? It all comes down to this business of loving, doesn't it? True love, a deep and sincere one, often leads us to do things which may seem strange to other people. Don't worry about them, Peta, I'm sure your beloved consultant knows what he's doing.'

Peta dried her hands on a fluffy new towel. There was sarcasm in Ashley's tone, a hint of disapproval of her obvious admiration for Dr Mandeville.

'It's marvellous how long some people can go on living on drugs,' he added, and then a regrettable silence ensued. Peta felt embarrassed and annoyed at his inference. There were nearly thirty years difference between her age and Ossy's. Surely Ashley didn't imagine that she was waiting for Mrs Mandeville to die so that she could step into her shoes?

It was unthinkable—yet she had thought it, although she was blaming Ashley for those thoughts. He hadn't said in so many words and he couldn't possibly know how she felt about Ossy. *Had* felt—yes, her lonely nights since living alone had frequently been occupied with such selfish fantasies. Both Dr and Mrs Mandeville had been kind to her, understanding her grief and loneliness, trying to help her through those early days when she had of necessity been forced to mature ahead of her years.

Those fantasies had stimulated the part of her which she felt had almost died. Now, since Ashley's arrival and meeting Quentin, she appreciated that the Mandevilles had merely taken her parents' place for a while. At nearly twenty-five she was beginning to experience changes in her life, emotional ones, and she knew that, much as she loved her work and was devoted to caring for her young patients in Angelique ward, she wanted to be married with children of her own.

'Thanks very much for supper,' she said politely. 'It was very nice.'

Ashley swung round from the display cabinet where he was packing away the plates.

'Christmas isn't over yet, Peta. This wasn't how you'd planned to spend it, I know. Your brother's telephone call and those few tears told me quite a bit about the Peta inside.' He grabbed her waist, probed with fingers and thumbs until she laughed. 'And where's your principal boy pantomime hat?'

'Quentin said I looked ridiculous in it,' she answered with a shaky voice.

'I thought you looked most becoming in it.' He pulled her towards him and she closed her eyes, expecting, wanting—but instead she felt his lips lightly brush her forehead. 'It's a bit late, and I think we're both too tired for party games, but young Neil told me that you'd challenged him to a game of chess, so how about getting some practice in?'

Half-way through the first game Peta wanted to laugh outright. Spending the late evening with Ashley had prevented her from feeling sorry for herself, but who would ever believe that they had spent it playing chess!

Losing to Ashley three times proved how out of practice she was and finally she insisted that she must go to bed.

'What sort of a day do you anticipate tomorrow?' Ashley asked as he saw her to the door.

'Plenty of visitors, I expect, and in the afternoon the staff give the first performance of their panto-mime, so we take as many of the children as we can to see it.'

'So it's no use my inviting you to accompany me down to Plymouth? Quentin suggested I ask you but, as I told him, it's a fairly hectic couple of days for the nursing staff. I know it's usual for those of you with no commitments to stand in to let the others off. Anyway, you can explain to Quentin yourself when he comes in to Gida's the next day.'

Peta felt irritated at the way Ashley had spoken for her. She said good night hurriedly and was glad to close her own front door where she could give vent to her anger in private.

Had he forgotten that she should really have been off duty all over the Christmas period? Or had he deliberately made excuses on her behalf because he was trying to keep her and Quentin apart?

Of course she had a hectic day in front of her, but she could have taken the day off. A whole day with Ashley and Quentin. Such an experience might have helped her to sort out her likes and dislikes of the two brothers. At this moment her preference was for Quentin. Ashley was taking too much upon himself deciding what was best for her. But after she had put out the light and lay in a state of drowsy consciousness, she acknowledged that Ashley did what he thought was best for her and had put himself out to be kind. She drifted happily off to sleep, recalling the snowball fight and the kisses . . .

The hospital seemed relatively quiet when Peta went on duty on Boxing Day morning. Quite a few of the doctors and nurses were feeling the effects of over-indulgence, which left a skeleton staff to do the vital jobs in the wards. As the day progressed the accident and emergency department became increasingly busy, with several casualties due to accidents on the icy roads and the elderly falling on slippery paths, as well as a few broken bones from sledging tumbles. But only one child, a little boy of five, was admitted to Angelique ward. He had severe lacerations around his mouth and eyes following the overturning of his and his brother's toboggan as they descended a steep bank on the nearby golf course.

Peta wheeled Neil along to the lecture hall to see the pantomime with all the other nurses from Angelique ward and their charges, and then she returned to stay and look after the few who were left, including the new admission, from whose parents she had to take all the particulars.

Little David Preston, who still had both legs suspended by a pulley, had his parents to keep him company and Paul Newton, who was making slow but definite progress, also had his mother and an older sister to tend his needs, so Peta could give her full attention to a very frightened Andrew Deakin.

He remained in the wheelchair, heavily bandaged and covered with a blanket just as the porter had left him, while Mr and Mrs Deakin sat in Peta's office trying to hide their nervousness.

'I can't promise the snow will last long enough for you to get better and get back to tobogganing,' Peta said with a reassuring smile to Andrew.

'I should think the boys will have had enough of tobogganing for a while,' Mrs Deakin said.

'Was it a Christmas present?' Peta asked as she selected the necessary admission forms.

Andrew nodded. He was beginning to look drowsy, so when the forms were completed she showed them to his bed and left them to see him safely tucked up.

Later on, during the early evening when the children had returned from the pantomime, had tea, been washed and settled for the night, Craig Murray sauntered into Peta's office.

'Gosh,' she greeted him, 'you look awful.'

His hair was tousled, his face unshaven. 'Mm— the morning after. I seem to remember dancing with you. Did I make a date or—anything?'

'No,' Peta laughed. 'You should be ashamed of yourself, Craig.'

'It *is* Christmas,' he muttered.

'So what's Hogmanay going to be like?'

'If I can remember anything afterwards I'll let you know,' he said, rubbing his bloodshot eyes. 'I'm just going off duty now, but I came to tell you that Andrew Deakin is down to see the eye specialist tomorrow if we can get hold of him. I'm fairly certain the wee laddie's going to be all right, but I'd rather he was checked right away.'

Craig went away with shuffling footsteps. Peta knew that he had been on call overnight and had been the victim of a drunk's abuse as well as having a steady stream of casualties to treat. She was pleased that at least he had enjoyed the Christmas Day parties and could now go off for some well-earned rest.

She was ready to leave as soon as Nicky came on duty. The roads were really treacherous now, the snow frozen hard and slippery, but she carefully picked her way along and managed to stay upright until she got to Mrs Hubbard's gateway, and then she slipped and fell on her bottom with a painful thud. She sat there for a second or two, then struggled to her feet, looking round and hoping no one was about.

Peta knew the old lady would worry if she told her she had fallen so she said nothing, but was grateful for the cup of tea and goodies Mrs Hubbard provided. She stayed chatting for nearly two hours and finally, after a glass of sherry, made her excuses and went home.

She soaked in a warm, scented bath and was in bed reading, which she liked to do in order to relax, when she heard Ashley come home. She prayed that he wouldn't ring her doorbell, even though she was curious as to how he had spent the day with Quentin. But tomorrow the decorations had to come down and she would see Quentin herself. New admissions would arrive ready for the next theatre list—it would be back to normal again.

With relief she heard the slam of his front door. She read on for ten minutes but realised that she hadn't taken in a word because she was straining her ears to hear movement from the downstairs flat. The last thing she remembered was hearing music coming from television or radio, and Ashley singing along with the carols heartily. He had evidently had an enjoyable day with his brother.

The Royal Marines arrived mid-morning and to Peta's disappointment there was no sign of Quentin. A sergeant appeared to be in charge and the job of removing the decorations was almost completed when Peta saw the two brothers coming briskly along the corridor, laughing together jovially.

Peta had just admitted a new case of suspected abdominal abscess, so she returned to her office to deal with the growing pile of paperwork. The two men paused a short distance away from the office door, evidently to finish the convivial chat which ended in masculine guffaws. Whatever had amused them had reduced them to two small boys again, Peta thought, and for the first time observed some closeness between them.

They came into her office still chortling with amusement.

'Do we all get to share the joke?' she asked, looking up from her desk.

'Not fit for innocent, delicate ears like yours, my dear,' Ashley said. His eyes were brimming with merriment and causing attractive creases to radiate from the corners.

'Sorry you couldn't make it to Plymouth yesterday, Peta,' Quentin said. 'You missed a good party.'

'It sounds like it, I'm intrigued,' she said.

'Quite a stag affair,' Ashley put in. 'These Army and Navy dos aren't fit for nice young ladies.'

'Come off it, old boy, there were almost equal numbers of the sexes,' Quentin divulged.

Ashley's expression turned quickly to his usual severe manner.

'Um—I thought you'd like to know I've just had

an emergency in my clinic. Young Marty Alexander again, so I'm admitting him at once and he'll be on my list later in the week.'

Peta's mouth dropped open with disappointment. He couldn't, he mustn't, she pleaded silently.

'It's not fair to the little chap to keep him hanging about any longer. Dr Mandeville was doubtful about letting him go home and he advised me to operate as and when I decided—and I've decided, much to the parents' relief.'

Peta wanted to argue with him but Quentin was present, so she remained silent, struggling for self-control, and then with a nod Ashley turned and left.

Quentin closed the office door behind him and then held Peta's chin in his hand and bent to kiss her.

'I'd forgotten how ravishing you are,' he whispered. 'But what's up? You look angry.'

'It's nothing,' Peta said blinking away the fury from her eyes. 'It's just this baby—'

'I'm only here for a few minutes. The men have all but finished and we have to rush back. A big three day exercise to organise to make use of this weather, but I shall be free on New Year's Day. Can I take you out to dinner?' Baby Alexander was momentarily forgotten as Quentin's persuasive charm made Peta's heartbeats quicken, and they made plans eagerly for January 1st of the New Year.

It was evident too, from Cathy's flushed cheeks, that she wasn't the only one with an exciting date to look forward to.

The ward seemed bare without the glittering decorations and ominously empty without the men of the Royal Marines, but all too soon Peta was worrying over Marty Alexander again. The young parents brought him to the ward from the out-patient clinic and stayed with him until early evening, when he was settled for the night.

Peta had to suppress her own thoughts about his condition. He had deteriorated in just the few days he'd been at home, so in her heart she knew that surgery was the only course left, but she wished that Ossy was there. She supposed it was just one more aggravation from Ashley, and she felt peeved that she had been proved wrong.

During the preliminary period of preparation preceding the operation, Marty was given small feeds of glucose-saline. Peta did everything herself and proceeded as usual for nursing sick babies up to the age of one year, when the danger of cross-infection is much greater than with older children.

On the day of the operation she put on a clean white gown and washed her hands thoroughly before putting on pre-packed sterile gloves to give Marty the necessary stomach washout. Then, to keep him warm, she wrapped his little limbs in cotton wool and, to prevent wriggling, bandaged him to a padded wooden splint in the shape of a cross by means of a figure of eight bandage round the shoulders, leaving the neck free from restriction and also the lower ribs. The lower part of the body and legs were also bandaged to the crucifix and then a blanket placed over him for added warmth.

Then she carried him to the anaesthetic room.

Ashley had just returned to the theatre after a mid-morning break. He came briskly into the anaesthetic room and looked at Marty, then he turned to Peta.

'I know you'll never forgive me for not waiting until Dr Mandeville is back, but it is *not* the first Ramstedt's operation I've performed. Why don't you stay?'

'I hadn't planned—' she started awkwardly.

'It only takes fifteen minutes. Telephone down to your staff nurse and then get scrubbed up.'

Peta glanced towards the theatre sister helplessly, but by her expression she indicated that she didn't mind, so Peta telephoned Cathy quickly and then went to get scrubbed up with the theatre sister.

It was a long while since she had assisted in the theatre and she felt nervous. She hoped Ashley wasn't going to make a point of airing their difference of opinion to the medical staff, but as the operation proceeded he explained in detail exactly how he was dividing the pyloric sphincter muscle.

'The cause,' he said, 'is not known. Sister Blair here has put up a valiant fight on Marty's behalf to avoid surgery by treating him with Eumydrin, an antispasmodic drug. But the wall of the pyloris has thickened, owing to a defect in the nervous-reflex mechanism, so that it doesn't open and close normally to allow the regular flow of food onwards as digestion proceeds. Vomiting has persisted since Marty was three weeks old. There has been only temporary improvement when he's in Sister Blair's tender care, so to save the little chap and the parents any further distress this operation became necessary. There was a danger of him becoming extremely ill from dehydration and starvation.'

Post-operative care was very important and Peta scarcely had time to go to lunch as she watched diligently over her small patient.

Ashley visited her during the afternoon and looked at Marty with pride.

'There we are,' he said triumphantly. 'No problems, and in a few weeks' time you won't recognise him.'

Peta wouldn't allow herself to show Ashley that she was ready to agree with him. She was all too mindful of the care Marty needed over the next few days, and she could only feel genuine sympathy for the little mite.

'I've looked out a feeding schedule we've used previously,' she said now to him confidently. 'Perhaps you'd have a look and make your comments, please.'

He put his hand under her elbow as she walked back to her office.

'I'm sure you've got it right, Peta,' he said with that same degree of sarcasm and patronage which was frequently evident in his tone.

'Not necessarily,' she retorted off-handedly. 'Your post-operative regime may differ from Dr Mandeville's.'

When he made no further comment as she handed him the details she had prepared, she dared to glance at his face and noticed his raised eyebrows and an almost impatient sigh which came from slightly parted lips.

She sat down at her desk and waited.

'Mm,' he murmured. 'Good. Avoid pressing on

with the schedule too quickly or the result will be irritation of the intestinal tract. Make sure the rest of the nursing staff understand this. I know you're going to be extra cautious with Marty.'

He handed back the schedule, waiting for her to make some reply, but she only muttered her thanks in a desultory voice.

Ashley moved towards the door, then turned. 'I suppose you're never ever going to forgive me for this?'

'Huh!' she replied indignantly. 'Who am I to forgive or not to forgive? I just hope everything turns out as you expect.'

'Have you some secret information which leads you to believe all will *not* be well?'

Peta shook her head.

'Don't be so damned stubborn, Peta!' The sudden exasperation in his voice made her realise that she had successfully tried his patience to the limit. She still felt that she could have continued treating Marty with medication until Ossy returned. She felt that Ashley had operated with indecent haste. Was he trying to prove to her and everyone at Gida's how efficient he was? There were plenty of other ways, she thought sourly, plenty of opportunities on new admissions to show his skills without pinching one of Ossy's patients.

'Marty's place is in his own home,' he stated adamantly. 'In my opinion enough time has been wasted, although I appreciate your reasons and your loyalty to Dr Mandeville. I hope you'll be able to find a little loyalty to spare for me? I don't have to remind you of the dangers of becoming over fond of someone else's child, surely?'

Peta flushed angrily, yet could not find words with which to express her fury.

'Mrs Alexander will be ringing me early this evening and I shall urge her to spend as much time as possible here to tend her own baby, under your expert supervision, of course,' he added, and with that he strode away.

Peta was still fuming when Nicky came on duty.

'He didn't have to be so blasted smug about doing a Ramstedt's on Marty Alexander,' she grumbled.

'But you did know it was on the cards,' Nicky said. 'And it's all over now, he'll probably make really good progress.'

'Oh, not you too! Does everyone have to see everything in terms of surgery?'

'Get off home, crosspatch,' Nicky teased. 'You know Ossy really wanted to let Mr Reeves operate, but you twisted him round your little finger. This one isn't going to be so easy to twist, Pet, and he might do us all good. Maybe we've become a bit too complacent with the easy-going Ossy.'

'I don't see what complacency's got to do with it,' Peta argued. 'He wasn't being easy-going because he didn't want to operate—just extra-cautious, caring. Trying to spare the parents any needless anxiety.'

'Only it hasn't—and you know that as well as the rest of us. It was unfortunate in my view that Marty responded to you and medication. If he hadn't he would have had the op at the start and would have been home for Christmas anyway. The parents aren't *so* stupid, Pet. They could have followed the feeding schedule with as much care as we do here.'

Peta sighed, expelling her breath so that a tendril of smokey-blonde hair curled upwards over her forehead against her white starched cap.

'Well,' she said flatly, 'he should be okay now.' She followed the list of patients down with her forefinger.

'The boys have to see the orthopaedic specialist at his clinic tomorrow with new sets of X-rays. Emma Brooks seems fine and I should think will be able to go home after Mr Reeves has seen her tomorrow. Paul Newton is beginning to show signs of recovery . . .' Peta continued through the report book methodically, giving Nicky full details of the new admissions, and for the first time in a long while she was glad to get out into the crisp night air.

The walk home cooled her temper. Had she really been coveting Marty Alexander? Such a thought alarmed her. She cared for all the children. She took her responsibilities seriously. If she saw a younger nurse being thoughtless towards a child she was quick to remind her that tender compassion was the first rule in nursing. A little sympathy went a long way, but only experience could teach how to show sympathy and combine it with the right amount of firmness. Babies were such helpless individuals, and you had to love them in order to nurse them back to health. Perhaps deep down she had missed the twins, Peter and Paul, and Bunty more than she realised. How would she cope with children of her own? She was reaching a quarter of a century, was she going to be denied that pleasure?

As she trudged along, realising that the bottom of her spine ached and was probably bruised from her fall earlier, she was extra-careful not to slip up again. Perhaps it was that which was the cause of her irritability and tonight she felt in no mood to visit Mrs Hubbard. Instead, she had a few words with her on the telephone, then tried a few gentle exercises to relieve the pressure on her spine before having a hot bath and going to bed, finding some relief from a hot water bottle at her back.

During the next two days she did her best to hide her discomfort. She knew she was doing all the right things but warmth, rest, hot baths, exercise and rubbing in liniment gave her only limited respite from the nagging ache which troubled her at night, and the excruciating pain she experienced when she got up from a sitting position.

When Cathy and Nicky quizzed her about it Peta assured them that she was treating herself, and that it was only the bruising taking extra long to come out—which she convinced herself that it was. But when Nicky announced that she was off for six nights and was giving a New Year's Eve party, Peta dreaded it. There was no way she could get out of it. She had considered it a good idea to help Nicky's parents so she had to support Nicky. The only trouble was that Nicky had invited Ashley Reeves too, who in turn offered to escort Peta.

It was a happy family occasion, nothing too ostentatious. They lived in a fair sized house about a mile out on the opposite side of town to Peta, and because there was no let-up in the bitterly cold weather Peta was glad of the lift to and from Nicky's house. She managed to remain on her feet most of the evening, dancing with Nicky's brother or idly chatting to Mr and Mrs Terry as she ate, but nothing would induce her to sit down and she hoped no one noticed. She was thankful, though, when the hands on the clock drew near to midnight. After the New Year had been toasted in to an unmusical version of *Auld Lang Syne* she looked hopefully towards Ashley.

'You look as if you've had enough,' he whispered, reaching her from the other end of the large lounge.

'I'm on duty tomorrow morning—*this* morning rather,' she said. 'I don't want to break up the party.'

'I doubt if Nicky's parents want the party to last for ever.' He took Peta by the hand and led her to Nicky, where they made polite excuses to leave.

It was such a relief to sit down in the car, but the cold seemed to penetrate right through to her bones and she shivered.

'I'm sorry I brought you away if you weren't in a hurry to leave,' she said.

'It was a good party, but you're on early shift.'

There was something in his voice that made her feel guilty. He had wanted to stay. She could have told him that Nicky would welcome him back again but she felt too miserable to even try to persuade him.

It seemed a never-ending drive and she longed to be on her own in her own flat, but when they drew up at last outside the house, Ashley ordered her to sit still.

'I'll open the gates,' he said, and when he had done that he drove a short distance into the drive, then stopped.

He was out and round to her side of the car before she could muster enough courage to even try to wriggle forward. He opened the door, put his hands beneath her knees and swivelled her round.

'No, please . . .' she began.

'I've seen a few bad backs in my time, Peta, had one myself in fact, so I know how painful it is. Put your feet outside the car. Now, lean on me and gently stand up.'

She couldn't help a cry of agonising pain as she lifted herself off the seat.

'I'll be all right,' she said quickly. 'It's just awkward getting up.'

'Got your key handy? Mind you don't slip, though I have put some sand down on the slippery places.'

He guided her up the path and as soon as she had opened the door he said, 'Now, upstairs, my girl and let's see what you've been up to.'

CHAPTER EIGHT

PETA tried to remonstrate. 'It's just—' she began.

'Just nothing—do as I say,' Ashley commanded, and followed her up the stairs after he had helped her off with her boots and slipped off his snowy shoes.

On the landing he took off his sheepskin coat and unwound the long scarf he always wore.

'I'll be all right,' Peta said for what seemed like the hundredth time.

'Yes, you will—presently.' He opened the door of the lounge and urged her inside. She took her coat off. 'And the rest,' he ordered sharply. Peta looked at him in astonishment and her mouth hung open, yet she was unable to voice the thoughts racing through her bemused head.

'For goodness sake, Peta. You don't really think I want to try anything on with you in that state? I've been watching you these past few days—you seem to be unaware that the pain shows in your face.'

'I . . . I slipped the other day outside Mrs Hubbard's,' she explained. 'I can't have done much damage, I can move my legs about normally.'

'I haven't specialised in children all my life,' he informed her brusquely, 'and thankfully I haven't forgotten all I learnt in Orthopaedics. Out in the jungle you need a bit of everything. Now, off with that dress and everything except the bare essentials, then get down on the floor.'

It was only afterwards that she looked back and giggled helplessly at the embarrassing incident. She with only bra and briefs on, covered with goose pimples until he, in shirt sleeves, ran expert fingers over her back before suddenly wrenching her fiercely. She had let out a cry and then he had knelt beside her and massaged her neck.

'Get yourself X-rayed tomorrow, then try to take a few days off until you're sure you're okay. You may need some follow up treatment. See someone in Orthopaedics.'

But Peta did not follow his advice. She could hardly believe that such swift, tortuous treatment could effect such an immediate remedy. Sitting, lying or standing was no problem the following day, and when she walked home from Gida's after a comparatively easy morning she decided to have a couple of hours rest before her dinner date with Quentin.

The quiet, relaxing afternoon did her good, though after a long luxurious bath she experienced a few twinges, so she had a cup of tea and took two strong pain-killers before making up her face and varnishing her fingernails in a shell-pink shade to match her lipstick and to complement the jade green wool dress and boxy jacket she had selected to wear. It suited her colouring and with its gold glitter thread in the weave was dressy enough for an evening out.

She was securing dainty gold studs in her ear-lobes when she heard the low sound of an engine purring outside and the crackle of tyres on the heaped, frozen snow in the gutter. She quickly drew back a corner of the heavy curtains, dropping it again at once when she recognised Ashley's Granada below.

Peta cursed under her breath. She had hoped they would have been on their way before he arrived home. She put out her bedroom light, leaving only the top landing one on. She always did that when she was out in the evenings. She waited, listening for any sound which might indicate that Ashley was putting his car away, but instead the loud peal of her doorbell made her jump. It had such an urgent, ominous ring and confused her conflicting thoughts even further. For a brief moment of guilt-ridden secrecy she thought that if she kept quiet he would give up and go away, but how foolish she would look if Quentin turned up, so she went downstairs and opened the door.

'Sorry if you were resting,' Ashley began, then his observing glance registered that she was dressed up.

'Oh—have you just come in or are you going out?' His brown eyes studied her critically, so she faltered before rushing on, talking too fast in an attempt to explain.

'I . . . I'm going out, yes, I have a date. A dinner date—with your brother.' She gulped, feeling hot and flusterd, but there was no point in beating about the bush, he might as well know the truth.

This appeared to completely floor him. He looked so terribly solemn, yet there was no trace of anger in his expression.

'You didn't go to Orthopaedics,' he accused. 'You haven't been X-rayed, which is very irresponsible.'

'But I'm so much better, and I am truly grateful to you.'

He swallowed hard. Peta couldn't believe that he was embarrassed at her words of gratitude.

'I'm afraid you won't be, Peta. I hesitated before ringing your bell, thinking you might be in bed, but the news I received today will probably come as something of a shock.'

She woke up to the fact that it must be bad news. Ivor? One of the children? But they would contact her here at home. Then it must be Quentin. She recalled him saying about the exercises. He must have had an accident.

'I've just heard that Mrs Mandeville had a severe stroke after only one day in Switzerland, and she died yesterday.'

Peta felt herself go cold and her skin prickled as she comprehended the tragic news.

'I'm sorry to have to spoil your evening, Peta, but I thought you'd want to know. Although one always clings to a last shred of hope, it was inevitable in her condition, and this, as it happens, was a nice way for her to end her days.'

'But he ought never to have taken her! I mean, expected her to cope with a long flight and—and—everything,' she blustered.

'I daresay Dr Mandeville knew all the risks, and I doubt that the journey had anything to do with it. She'd been fighting her illness for some time. Such intense treatment must eventually take its toll, and once she reached the place she loved she gave up the struggle.' Ashley reached out and touched her arm with gentle reassurance. 'It was best this way, Peta,' he added sympathetically.

She stood there gazing stupidly at him while he unlocked his door, and suddenly she wanted, needed him—but at that moment a luxurious red Volvo came into the Crescent and drew up behind Ashley's car.

'Ah, here's Quentin,' Ashley said. 'It's a good thing you have a date tonight. There's nothing anyone can do for Dr Mandeville, so try to put it to the back of your mind for a while.'

'Hello there—all set?' Quentin greeted cheerfully.

'Make sure you wear a warm coat,' Ashley advised and Peta retraced her steps back up to her own flat, where she needed a few minutes to collect her thoughts.

She felt deep compassion for Ossy. He was such a dear man, a true friend, a faithful husband and she knew he would be shattered even though his wife's death had been expected.

It didn't seem right to be going out to enjoy herself with Quentin. Yet as Ashley said, there was nothing she could do—nothing anyone could do, except offer up a silent prayer for the strength and courage the much loved consultant was going to need in the coming days.

Peta could hear the twin brothers talking. Ashley was obviously explaining all the details to Quentin. After she had put on a three-quarter length simulated fur coat and returned to the porch, Quentin turned to her with concern.

'Are you sure you're up to coming out, Pet? Didn't you ought to stay in the warm?'

She realised that Ashley had also told his brother about her back.

'I'm fine,' she assured him, 'really. I've been to work this morning, and I'm off all day tomorrow, so I can take it easy then. I'm grateful to Ashley for putting it right so promptly.'

'It's early days yet, so take care,' Ashley answered. 'Have a good evening anyway,' and he went inside and closed the door.

Peta pulled her front door behind her and turned the key in the lock. Quentin closed the outer door, then held her arm as she walked carefully out to the car.

The next few minutes were awkward while Peta struggled with emotion over the demise of Mrs Mandeville. Quentin was saying all the correct things and at the same time trying not to sound too gloomy, but once they reached the Royal Oak Inn, a rather select place renowned for its cosy, romantically inclined atmosphere as well as superb food, they steered the conversation to lighter topics.

A huge log fire burned in an outsized fireplace in the lounge bar, where Quentin bought cocktails, an appetiser to the three course dinner which they leisurely chatted over. The large restaurant was hexagonal in design and Quentin and Peta occupied one of the six, two-tabled alcoves which surrounded the main body of the restaurant.

Christmas decorations were still very much in evidence and in the centre of each table was a posy made up of holly, ivy and scarlet poinsettias with a white candle in the centre. Its flame reminded Peta of a tear-drop upside down, and in a quiet moment she gazed into the golden light and thought of Mrs Mandeville. There would be no more dinner parties at their home, and no more match-making

It was like peering into a crystal ball. She saw herself and Ashley, feeling his gentle, manipulative hands gliding over her spine, sensing the soothing delight of his touch—then, through the flame she saw Quentin smiling and she laughed back at him, her acute hearing responding to his compliment.

'You're looking lovelier than ever tonight, Pet. I must be the envy of every man in this restaurant.'

'Tell me about your exercises,' she invited, and for the next hour Peta was kept amused at Quentin's adventures, both recent and in the past.

After coffee, liqueuers and mint chocolates it was time to go. The drive back to Vandyke Crescent took half an hour, and Peta was at the point of inviting Quentin in for more coffee when he switched off the car's engine and turned to look at her as he undid his safety belt.

'We must do this again,' he said, and kissing her lightly on her lips released the catch on her belt. 'I've no doubt old Ash is in there pretending to be asleep, but watching the clock to see how late I kept you.'

'It's only ten past twelve,' Peta said, glancing at the clock on the dashboard. 'And it's got nothing to do with Ashley where I go, who I go with or how late I stay out.'

'Only a fool would stay out unnecessarily in such icy weather,' Quentin said before he kissed her again. Then he opened his door, got out and walked round the front of his gleaming Volvo to open Peta's door and help her out.

Peta opened the porch door and again was about to invite him in when he slid his hands beneath her coat, drew her up against him and kissed her swiftly but fiercely. His fingers hovered delicately, almost irritatingly, around her waist and then he said good night and returned to his car.

Peta's spirits suffered the anti-climax stoically. It was only their first real date. What had she expected of him? She lifted her hand in farewell as he raised his and drove on round the Crescent.

The street was so quiet, the sky almost dark blue with the reflection of snow eerily silhouetting roofs and chimney pots. A crescent moon and a thousand stars winked mystically down at her. They were like sparklers; was there one for every human she wondered? One somewhere for Mrs Mandeville, she was sure.

She watched Quentin's rear lights disappear. Then she noticed Mrs Hubbard's front room light showing through the curtain. Now what was she doing, reading until this hour! Peta smiled wistfully. Probably the old lady was fast asleep and the book had long dropped on to the carpet. It had happened many times before, she knew.

She was about to close her own front door when a pitiful wail echoed from across the street. Peta hesitated. Snudgie? He was usually out all night but seldom made weird noises. The cry came again, and again. Instinct told Peta something was wrong. Was he hurt perhaps? Or had Mrs Hubbard put him out earlier than usual and dropped off to sleep before giving him his supper? It was mad to go investigating a cat's cries at this time of night, but some sixth sense urged her to close her door again, and carefully tiptoeing across the glassy surface of the road in her high heels she managed to get safely over to the other side.

Peta followed the cries and found Snudgie with his nose up tight against the front door, which was at the side of the house.

'What's the matter with you?' she whispered. 'Too cold for even you to be out tonight? You don't usually make such a hullaballoo—didn't she give you any supper?'

Peta walked on round the side of the house to the back door and saw that the kitchen light was on and the curtains drawn back. That was unusual. She'd expect to find it like that in the morning, but as soon as evening drew in Mrs Hubbard always closed all her curtains.

Peta went back to where the cat was still mournfully wailing. She called through the letterbox.

'Mrs Hubbard? Are you still up? Mrs Hubbard?'

Fortunately the door curtain had been pulled back so Peta bent down and peered through the letterbox. Her vision was limited but as she twisted awkwardly because of the ache at the base of her spine, she finally saw part of the old lady's ankle and slippered foot curled round at the bottom of the stairs.

'Mrs Hubbard? Can you hear me?' Peta called loudly, but there was no response.

'Oh, God—what do I do now?' Peta said aloud.

She had no key. Mrs Hubbard was an independent soul who refused to allow anyone admission to her home without invitation. It was no use anyway, for even if she'd had a key Peta felt sure the safety chain would be secured. She'd have to go for help, and she mustn't waste time. Somehow she hurried back to her own flat without slipping up, then remembered that Ashley might still be up. But there were no lights on anywhere, so she rang his bell and banged on the front windows.

He, who was always so interested in all her comings and goings was now fast asleep when she needed his help she supposed. Just like a man!

'Ashley, Ashley,' she called, but he probably couldn't hear because the windows were all double glazed. She rang the bell and let it ring for several seconds, then called once more, this time through the letter-box.

A light showed through the curtains at last. Peta could hear murmurings getting closer, then the front door opened.

'What's the matter?' he growled.

'It's Mrs Hubbard,' Peta said in an urgent whisper. 'I think she's on the floor unconscious. It was the cat crying which attracted my attention.'

'Decent folk are in bed and asleep,' he grunted, pulling his trousers on over his pyjamas and shrugging into his sheepskin jacket.

'You . . . you can't come out like that,' she said suddenly, 'it's freezing.'

He ignored her, put his keys in his pocket and closed the door.

'It's all my fault,' Peta began as they stepped cautiously over the icy ruts of snow in the road.

'Don't start blabbering, for heaven's sake. Let's see what we find first.'

Peta picked up the cat and buried her face in his fur coat while Ashley peered through Mrs Hubbard's letterbox. He straightened up, then turned to Peta.

'Go home and call the police and ambulance, while I see if I can get in round the back.'

Peta hesitated. For a moment she felt her place was with the old lady.

'Go on,' urged Ashley, 'and take the cat with you.'

But Snudgie struggled to get down. No way was he going to leave his mistress and his patch.

Peta did as she was told, giving the address and details clearly to the services, and then she went back across the road once again.

Ashley had climbed up on to the kitchen window sill.

'Do be careful,' Peta urged with concern. 'I expect it's all closed.'

'This fanlight isn't secure.' Ashley jumped down and began to take off his coat.

'You'll catch your death,' Peta yelled at him.

'Hold it and shut up. It's too bulky,' Ashley replied shortly.

He climbed up again, pulled out the fan-light and, while propping it up with his head, reached down and undid the latch on the casement window. In a matter of minutes he was inside and Peta heard him draw back the bolts and unlock the back door.

'Hot water bottle and blankets, Peta,' he ordered as he went at once to where the old lady was lying in the hall.

It seemed ages, but could only have been five minutes later that they heard the sound of cars outside. Police and ambulance arrived simultaneously while Ashley and Peta both rubbed Mrs Hubbard's limbs in an effort to get the blood flowing again. She did at last open her eyes when she was snugly wrapped up on the stretcher with a hot water bottle between the blankets.

'Look after Snudgie,' she croaked in a frightened voice.

'Of course I will, Mrs Hubbard,' Peta said, 'and don't worry, you're going to be all right.'

Peta wanted to go with her but Ashley dissuaded her, so after giving the ambulancemen some particulars she then gave full details to the police.

'Someone should have a key,' one of the constables said. 'She's pretty well barricaded in—thankfully one window was insecure. Good job you were around, sir,' he said to Ashley. 'The young lady wouldn't have been able to reach the catch on the casement window.'

'Long arms come in useful sometimes,' Ashley said and took his coat from Peta and put it on.

They stayed chatting for a while and Peta agreed to take any tins of cat food she could find in order to care for Snudgie, who they found in the kitchen washing himself after eating the plateful of food Mrs Hubbard had left down.

'He's got his own basket and blanket,' Peta said, 'so I'll take those over with me, though I know he's nocturnal and doesn't usually stay in at night.'

'Animals sense when something's wrong and they adapt well as long as they're fed regularly,' the policeman said. 'Could we leave a key with you, miss? No doubt you'll be visiting Mrs Hubbard in hospital as you're on hand. There's sure to be things she'll need, and you can keep the place dry and aired in case she ever comes back.'

'Don't let Mrs Hubbard hear you suggest she won't,' Peta said indignantly.

'She's done well for turned eighty,' the policeman replied, 'but it can't go on for ever.'

'She's very independent, and more able than most of her age,' Peta said in defence of Mrs Hubbard.

The policeman raised his eyebrows. 'Until she fell and couldn't get up. This weather doesn't give cases like this much chance. She's the fourth since Christmas.'

Peta was shivering herself. Evidently Mrs Hubbard must have fallen quite early that morning. There was no heating on anywhere, and she had been in her nightdress and dressing-gown, both of which were thick, which had probably saved the old lady's life.

The police locked up the house and Snudgie gave them all a disdainful look and ran off into the night. Ashley helped Peta carry the basket and some tins of food across to number fifty-six.

'I'll leave it here in the hall for now,' Peta said. Then, turning to Ashley who had followed her in, she suddenly felt weak at the knees and in need of a good cry. When she tried to thank him for all that he had done she broke down. He took her in his arms and held her close to him, allowing her to weep freely.

'Come along, darling,' he soothed, 'upstairs in the warm.'

'You must be chilled,' she managed to say.

'That's why we're going to warm up by your gas fire and have a tot of brandy for medicinal purposes—or whisky if you have either.'

'Both,' she said.

'Ah—so that's your secret!'

'For medicinal purposes,' she said and laughed through her tears.

Upstairs in Peta's lounge she found the brandy and glasses in the cupboard while Ashley lit her gas fire. Then he went into her bedroom and switched on her electric blanket.

'Just as well you were wearing your fur coat,' he told her, standing close beside her and taking the glass from her trembling fingers. She found the strength of him as he drew her against himself comforting, and yet she knew her weeping was not over.

'First Mrs Mandeville, now Mrs Hubbard . . .' and she buried her face in her handkerchief again.

'Mrs Hubbard's going to be all right,' he whispered into her hair, 'though it's only fair to warn you that she does probably have a fractured femur.'

'I guessed,' Peta sobbed, 'by the way she was lying.'

Peta didn't notice though that Ashley had removed his jacket, and now as he turned her round and slid her coat off her shoulders the sight of him in his pyjama jacket made her feel peculiar. His dark hair was very tousled and his chin dark and stubbly with a day's growth of beard, but masculine potency emanated from every pore of his strong, virile body.

He drew her nearer to the fire and lifted her chin to gaze at her tear-stained cheeks. She almost couldn't bear his scrutiny, and yet she needed his companionship.

'I'm sorry I had to disturb you,' she said.

The flicker of a smile creased the corners of his mouth.

'I'm glad you did.' His deep voice held some emotion she hadn't yet discovered in him, and then he pulled her hard against him, and his lips explored every inch of her face before finally settling over her half-open mouth. Half-open because she knew some little voice was urging her to protest, but as his demanding tongue engaged hers all thoughts of ethical behaviour dissolved. She had never doubted his physical strength, but now she was aware of the compelling hardness of his manhood as he sought to weaken her still further.

Was it the brandy going to her head, or his powerful influence? She felt herself go limp in his arms as heat and desire soared through her veins.

With a sighing groan he pushed her away.

'How's the back?' he asked huskily, and her liquid gaze met his smouldering inquisition with blatant appetite. Oh, for more of his massaging, she thought wistfully. But she answered quickly, 'Fine—a bit achy—but nothing to worry about.'

'You *will* worry—if I have to come up here and lift you out of bed one of these mornings,' he warned, and he was back to being the dominant Ashley Reeves. 'Just see that you get X-rayed before the week's out.'

'I'm off tomorrow,' she said feebly.

Did she—was she hoping that he'd remain here with her until reality came in with the dawn? A reality she was trying to postpone. The realisation that Mrs Mandeville had died, and that Mrs Hubbard, such an old and trusted friend, was lying in a hospital bed injured.

She might have prevented that if she had gone over earlier to see her instead of feeling sorry for herself over a few back pains, and excited anticipation of her date with Quentin.

That all seemed a decade ago. What had happened during the past hour had more than made up for the feeling of anti-climax she had felt when Quentin brought her home. She had expected more, so much more from him, but it was Ashley who had roused a surging passion within her.

'See that you spend it wisely then,' Ashley was saying now. 'Have a really good rest; no trying to do housework either for yourself or Mrs Hubbard, and no lifting, of course.'

'I shall go in to see Mrs Hubbard,' Peta said.

'There's no need. I'll see her and tell her you're looking after Snudge, and assure her that we'll guard her property between us.'

'But I must, I want to,' Peta insisted.

'I said *no!*' This was the side of him which roused her, not to sexual passion but anger.

'If I want to go I will,' she contradicted.

'And I'm ordering you to stay at home and rest. I'll give you a certificate if that will help.'

'Thanks, but no thanks. I'll decide whether I need to rest or not.'

'I shall see the SNO first thing in the morning and tell her no more duty until you've been X-rayed and examined by Orthopaedics.'

'You are an interfering old—'

'I know,' he replied pompously, pulling himself up to his full height and looking incredibly sexy in his striped pyjama top. 'I don't mind what you call me, Peta, if it gets rid of your hang-ups.'

'Hang-ups!' she shot at him.

'Yes, darling. Grief over Mrs Mandeville, guilt over Mrs Hubbard, but you can't take everyone's burdens on your shoulders. And then there's the frustration.'

'Frustration!' She was equally as angry with herself as with him. She was normally quite good at verbal battles when sufficiently roused, but now that he was belittling her, all she could do was repeat his words.

'Why would I be frustrated, for goodness' sake?' she demanded hotly.

'Well you certainly haven't been satisfied, I've just proved *that*,' he said smugly. 'Quentin not up to his usual philandering self?'

Peta's cheeks burned at his mockery and she hated herself, and him, for the subtle way he had extracted what he wanted to know about her date with his brother.

'Good night, darling, sleep well, and remember, if you don't get your back checked I shall do it personally.' He had the gall to pat her cheek before picking up his coat and returning to his own flat.

CHAPTER NINE

PETA fumed, and even managed to consume the rest of the brandy left in her glass. She banged around the flat in disgust, but as she lay in bed later, and calmer now, she saw it all in a different light. Ashley Reeves had only tried to prove that he was as confident with women as Quentin was. Skilful too, she thought with dry humour. She would have been quite happy to have some more personal treatment from him.

She thought of Quentin who could make her laugh so easily. He was a fun companion, but he didn't turn her on. Whereas Ashley could devastate her with just one kiss, as she so well remembered from the incident under the mistletoe. She tried ticking off their differing qualities in her mind's eye and, like counting sheep, it worked magically. The next thing she knew was the telephone ringing, bringing her out of a deep sleep. Peta groaned. It was just after eight-thirty so she guessed who would be on the line.

'If it isn't too late, Pet, happy New Year,' Ivor said. 'As I rang you on Christmas morning I thought you might have telephoned us yesterday, but I rang you and there was no reply. Busy having a good time, I hope, lots of parties and plenty of excitement?'

Peta bristled indignantly. He made her sound like a good-time girl.

'Actually, I'm off today with a bad back,' she said self-pityingly, at which her brother roared with laughter.

'It's not funny, I can tell you,' she retorted crossly.

'Sorry, Peta—but, you know, that evokes a few suggestions.'

'Well it may to you, but to me it means pain.'

'Aah,' he drawled in sympathy. 'Is it really bad?'

She went on to tell him about her fall, making quite a thing of it until he suggested coming down to fetch her back to Brighton where they could look after her.

'I'd never be able to stand the journey,' she said.

'Well, I'd better come anyway,' he replied brightly.

'No—no—there's nothing you can do. I'm being very well cared for, and treated, and now there's Mrs Hubbard to worry about.'

She prattled on, getting into quite a state as she endeavoured to avoid mentioning Ashley by name. Instead she called him 'the new tenant downstairs.'

For once Ivor sounded interested. He allowed her to talk at length, then with a note of suspicion in his voice said, 'Seems to me Mr Fitzgerald did a good job finding a medical man to look after you.'

For a few seconds Peta was speechless. Then in a small voice she asked, 'How did you know about Mr Reeves?'

'My dear Pet, you don't imagine we'd agree to just anyone sharing the family home?'

'But it's self-contained flats now.'

'And jolly nice ones by all accounts. Of course, we didn't imply we preferred a professional man, a bachelor, but we felt you needed a man about the house. It's not large enough for a family, and a middle-aged or elderly couple might have been nosy or interfering. This surgeon chap sounds just the right type.'

There was an ominous silence between them while Peta talked herself out of blowing her top.

'Old Fitzgerald seemed to be taking his time,' Ivor hurried on to explain, 'and it so happens that a golfing friend of mine has this brother in the Marines who knew of the trouble his mate was in to find accommodation for his surgeon brother coming from—oh—somewhere or other.'

'Africa,' Peta put in bluntly.

'Well, it couldn't fail could it? Surgeon and nurse—bound to get on.'

Peta drew her breath in deeply.

'I was glad of his help tonight,' she admitted, 'but don't you think I see enough of medical staff all day and every day? And as to needing a man to look after me,' she said on another long, indrawn breath, 'I'm quite capable of finding one for myself.'

'Oh dear. Isn't it working out?'

'You think a middle-aged or elderly couple would be nosy and interfere? You should hear *him*!'

'It's early days yet, Pet. Give it time and I'm sure you'll both settle down and understand each other. When your back is better you must come down and spend some time with us.'

'When my back is up to the journey, and when all the snow has disappeared,' she agreed.

She remembered to ask about their Christmas,

and how Ros and the children were before he rang off.

Peta folded her arms and paced angrily. She ought to have known that big brother Ivor would have been behind letting the flat. Damn and blast him, she cursed inaudibly, as well as a few oaths she'd never dare utter in anyone else's presence.

She put the kettle on and while she waited for the water to boil she walked from one room to another feeling trapped. That patronising pig of a man downstairs—it was all *his* fault she declared. But a few minutes later, with pillows and a hot water bottle at her back as she sat up in bed to drink her tea, she acknowledged that her anger was misdirected.

Ashley was a victim of circumstance, only he wasn't so much the victim as she. How could they ever be compatible when he was so impossible both at home and at Gida's? They were too involved in the same pattern of life. Well, he wouldn't be around for ever if what he said was true—that he intended to return to Africa. And the sooner he went the better, she decided bitterly.

She was quite happy to rest in bed for most of the morning. There was so much on her mind. She desperately tried to read more into her evening out with Quentin. He wasn't the least bit bossy, but neither was he as demanding as she had anticipated he would be, which brought her back persistently to Ashley again, and the way he toyed with her emotions. His kisses left an indelible imprint on her lips. His touch, even the memory of his fingers caressing her, brought the blood in her veins to the boil. Somehow she had to show him that she could do without his attention, that she preferred Quentin's, but *he* hadn't committed himself to further meetings.

Her mind wandered and she felt a pang of grief when she thought of dear Ossy. Was he on his way home? Would he return to Gida's after a time of mourning? It all seemed so uncertain, just as Mrs Hubbard's future did . . .

Golly! She had forgotten Snudge. By now he was probably screaming at the door for breakfast. She got up as speedily as her back would allow, dressed in warm trousers and an extra-thick sweater over a polo-necked one, and went down to the front door.

The street seemed deserted and she glanced both ways before calling the cat's name several times. Then she tried a pathetic attempt at whistling, something she'd never been good at, and to her surprise Snudge leapt over Mrs Hubbard's front wall and scampered across the road, rushing straight through Peta's doorway as if he knew what was expected of him.

By the end of the day Peta and Snudgie were close buddies. The cat seemed to have an insatiable appetite, with brief playing or sleeping spells in between. He accepted that his basket was there for the latter and by late evening Peta was quite sorry when he asked to go out. He was quite a little character, a good companion.

She laughed as she recalled how she'd made fun of spinsters and their cats in the past. No doubt brother Ivor would say she was turning out just as he'd predicted. Is that why he had made a point of finding a tenant for the downstairs flat? Obviously they wanted to marry her off—anyone would do as long as *they* wouldn't have to be responsible for her in her old age, she supposed.

Mrs Mandeville had made no secret of her efforts to find Peta a husband. Peta sighed. Now she was gone and dear Ossy was alone. In the past Peta had dreamed dreams of a life shared with her idol, but now she realised that those fantasies had been more of a father-daughter relationship than one with any lover-like possibilities. Peta knew that he had a housekeeper, and in time she envisaged that he would come to terms with his sorrow, find some sophisticated professional woman and marry again.

She sighed as she prepared her things for duty next day. Here she was, leading a full life in so many ways, yet it was a solitary one. One thing was certain, she could do without Ashley Reeves poking his nose into everything she did.

After her day off she was on late shift the following day, which gave her a couple of hours in the morning to attend to her feline friend, go across to Mrs Hubbard's house, pick up any mail and drain all the water off. While the police had been there they had turned all the main supplies off and after a brief word with a plumber who was a family friend Peta did as she was advised and drained the system completely.

The weather was bright and still bitterly cold, so she decided against using the car yet. Instead she opened the garage, started up the engine and let it run for several minutes. Ashley's car was missing. Thank goodness he had gone to work and left her in peace. She unlocked the chest freezer which was housed in the garage and took out chops, chicken pieces and sausages with a packet of mixed frozen vegetables to transfer to her fridge in the flat, and then it was time to start her walk to Gida's hospital.

At some time she had to visit the orthopaedic ward to see Mrs Hubbard who, she had learned from a telephone enquiry the previous afternoon, was settling in despite the acute pain she had to endure. Traction was helping though, until she was well enough to have the fractured thigh-bone pinned. After that it would be a geriatric ward, and . . . Peta tried not to look too far ahead. It was sad to be alone in the world with no relatives except a couple of elderly cousins living in widely different parts of the country.

Almost as soon as she took charge of Angelique ward it was time to serve lunch, and in the middle of this Margaret Astley-Brown came through the door.

'How are you feeling, Sister Blair?' she asked.

Peta looked at her nonplussed. 'I'm fine,' she said.

'Mr Reeves reported that you fell and hurt your back.' The SNO smiled and raised her eyebrows knowingly.

Peta felt the colour stain her cheeks with indignation.

'He had no business to worry you over such a triviality,' she said, affronted.

'Oh, but he had. My nurses are my responsibility, Sister,' Matron said with a grin. 'Actually, Peta,' she added on a more familiar note, 'we were discussing poor old Mrs Hubbard and he just mentioned your problem.'

Peta wished she could magic away the persistent flush as she remembered Ashley's instant cure.

'It really isn't a problem, it's fine now.'

'I believe he ordered you to be X-rayed, and have a check-up in Orthopaedics? I'm afraid I'm bound to support that recommendation, Peta, for your own good.'

'Do I have to?' Peta pleaded.

Margaret's eyes danced with laughter in her usual happy manner, but her expression also held a firmness which Peta knew was useless to argue with.

'I've advised both departments, so they'll be expecting you. Get down to X-ray as soon as you can, then report to Orthopaedics late afternoon.' She turned to Cathy who was assisting Peta with lunches. 'Staff Nurse Hunter, see that Sister Blair doesn't go lifting the older children and make sure she does as I've said. You can manage, can't you?'

'You're conspiring against me,' Peta bemoaned. 'He'll have to go.'

'Don't say that, Pet,' Margaret laughed. 'With Ossy away, we can't do without him!'

'I meant out of my flat,' Peta corrected. Then with a change of mood she said, 'I was so sorry to hear about Mrs Mandeville. I know she looked ghastly at Christmas but she still sounded eager to go to Switzerland.'

Margaret sighed. 'Maybe that's what she was living for, and having reached her goal she simply gave up the fight. It often happens that way. I agree it's very sad for Mr Mandeville. Such a devoted couple. He won't be back for some considerable time. She asked to be buried out there on the mountainside in the churchyard of the little village she loved so much. Next Sunday afternoon we're having a memorial service for her in the hospital chapel. Naturally you and Cathy must be there and as many of Angelique's nurses as possible—I'll find one or two relief nurses for that hour. We thought Sunday was best as most of the mums will be here with the children. I was going to ring you, Peta, but when Mr Reeves said you were resting I decided to wait until you came in. I didn't want to get you out of bed.'

A gloom seemed to spread through Gida's over the next few days in anticipation of the service on Sunday.

Peta's troubles seemed so minor compared with the consultant's, but she dutifully had her back X-rayed, and was examined by the orthopaedic surgeon. After similar treatment to that of Ashley's she was pronounced in good shape.

Once more the children's needs occupied her working hours and much of her thoughts. When she was off duty she visited Mrs Hubbard, who was quickly transferred to a geriatric convalescent home after a successful operation and was surprising everyone by her determination to get on her feet and home again. Peta kept the old lady's home aired and clean as well as caring for the cat, which gave her little time to herself. In consequence she hardly saw Ashley until late one afternoon, when Peta was discussing Marty Alexander's excellent progress with his parents, she heard slow but solid footsteps enter the ward and turned to discover Ashley coming towards her with an elegant woman by his side.

'Good afternoon, Sister, Mr and Mrs Alexander,' he greeted with a nod. Then, with his hand under his companion's elbow, he drew her forward. 'I'd like to introduce you to a former colleague of mine, Dr Palmer, who is a paediatrician. I've been telling her all about young Marty here.'

'We're so grateful to you, Mr Reeves,' Mrs Alexander said. 'We can't wait to get him home now.'

'And what does Sister Blair think about that?' Ashley asked, looking directly at Peta.

She was so annoyed at his arrogance that she felt like telling him she wasn't paid to think, only to carry out his orders; instead she held her head proudly and replied, 'He's responded beautifully, so I should think any day now. He had his stitches removed on the tenth day, which was yesterday.'

Mr Alexander, a young, rather shy man, then surprised Peta by saying, 'We're more than grateful to you, Sister Blair. He couldn't have had better, more loving care anywhere than you've given him. I'm only worried that he's going to pine for you when he leaves.'

'I suspect Marty will get over the parting quicker than Sister Blair,' Ashley said with sarcasm, 'but don't worry, she's got a cat at home now, that will take Marty's place.'

This was received with much amusement although Peta felt like giving Ashley a sly kick. The trouble was, this Dr Palmer was standing between them. Peta was aware of her critical appraisal as well as the whiff of an expensive perfume which mingled with all the other baby smells. She was about the same height at Peta, perhaps slightly taller, with rich, ebony coloured hair, a tanned complexion and bright red lips to match the red silk scarf which showed at the neck of a belted tweed coat. Tenerife flashed into Peta's brain—was this who he had been trying to avoid? By the self-satisfied expression on his face Peta decided she must have it all wrong. As if she cared, anyway.

'I'll getch Marty's feed,' she said to the Alexanders who visited at this time of day in order to tend their baby son themselves and tuck him up for the night.

When Peta returned it was evident that Ashley had been telling his doctor friend about Marty's case history in detail.

'Our Sister here gave him her full attention and hoped to avoid surgery. But I think you agree now that it was right to operate?' he asked Peta.

'I'm glad the responsibility of such a decision didn't rest with me,' Peta answered quietly, and turned her attention to the baby in the next cot who was suffering from pneumonia. He was a recent admission, his mother an unmarried girl of seventeen who refused to give her baby up, and was doing her best to bring him up alone. She didn't have much to offer him except the most important thing of all, her love, and there was no shortage of that.

Ashley led Dr Palmer to each cot, following Peta, demanding her attention to the discussions they held over each case.

It was later when she was writing her report that a terrifying thought crossed Peta's mind. Was Ossy leaving Gida's for good?

It was almost ten o'clock when she turned into Vandyke Crescent. Thick clouds were scudding across the sky and the temperature was evidently rising, though not sufficient yet to melt the hard-packed ice and snow. Where sand and grit had been put down the streets looked unsightly, and Peta thought longingly of a warmer climate. For the remainder of the day since Ashley's visit to the ward, she had experienced an empty despondency in the pit of her stomach.

She felt in need of some hot sunshine and vaguely wondered if the idea of nursing abroad was such a bad one after all. She was loath to admit that she couldn't bear to see Ashley Reeves with another woman. Perhaps he was about to get married; maybe Dr Palmer was the special woman he had once talked about. Well, hadn't she wanted him out of the flat? Was she ready now to sell up, and make some of those teenage pipe dreams, which had seemed so mad at the time, come true? America? Canada? Why not get away as far as she could to Australia or New Zealand?

She was banging her feet on the ground and scraping the soles of her boots on the metal scraper when she heard a car purr to a halt at the gate. She turned and saw that Ashley had returned, so she went to open the outside wrought iron gates for him to save him getting out. As she glanced up she saw that he was helping a passenger out of the car.

'Thanks, Peta,' he called.

'Sorry, perhaps you're not bringing it in?' she replied awkwardly.

'Yes, I am, but Aileen is cold so she can let herself into the flat while I put the car away.'

Aileen was cold! Peta had been glowing after the walk home but now she froze up inside. So Aileen was staying with him!

'Mind how you go, darling,' he said to Dr Palmer

and then to Peta, 'Come and have a night-cap with us, Peta?'

Peta fought with her conscience. She was seething; how dare he bring his woman home to share the flat! He was only a tenant, after all, and her parents wouldn't approve of such goings on. For heaven's sake, don't be such an old killjoy, she chided herself.

'It's a bit late and I'm on split shift tomorrow,' she said, 'which means an early start.'

'No excuse,' came the blunt reply. 'You won't be going to bed for another hour at least.'

'I've got the cat to feed.'

'Do it afterwards.'

By now Peta had reached her front door and was answering him coolly over her shoulder. The lady doctor seemed to be having some difficulty in finding the right key on a sizeable bunch so Peta tried to help, and they had just managed it between them when Ashley joined them. Aileen went in first and Peta moved over to her own door, but Ashley placed very firm hands at her waist and forced her into his flat.

'Look, I . . .' she began in trepidation.

'Get your coat off, make yourself at home.' He laughed good-humouredly. 'Oh, of course, you are at home.' Then as he took her coat and hung it on the pegs on the wall he added, 'How's the back? I heard you were a good girl and did as I told you.'

'Has he been bullying you, Peta?' Aileen asked.

'He tries to,' Peta answered flatly, 'but he won't always succeed.'

'It's better to be safe than sorry, my dear,' he said, urging her forward to follow Aileen into his lounge. 'As it happens you were lucky. By treating you quickly we cleared up the trouble immediately, but so many people fall, pick themselves up, think they're only mildly bruised and do nothing more until months later when they're in agony. Now, what will you have? Martini, sherry?'

'A very *small* Martini,' Peta said, hating Ashley Reeves for bringing her into this situation. He handed her the drink, pausing to stare at her, but Peta averted her gaze and despised him even more when he rubbed his hands together gleefully and turned to Aileen. 'The usual for you, darling?'

'I'll have a Martini too, I think,' Aileen said, and with her coat over her arm went along the hall to the bedrooms. But which one, Peta found herself asking. Ashley's? Or the smaller one along the passageway?

Aileen had closed the lounge door so there was no way of telling. Peta felt like drinking her Martini in one gulp and dashing off.

'Relax, Peta, you seem all het up.'

'I'm thinking about the cat—and I am rather tired. There's been a lot to see to with Mrs Hubbard in hospital.'

'She's doing fine I believe, and she's a lucky lady to have you to look after things.'

He almost pushed her down into the nearest chair and when Aileen returned a few minutes later she was wearing a thick cardigan over the grey and red woollen dress. She had also changed from her sheepskin-lined boots into casual shoes, and suddenly Peta realised how strange this flat seemed to her now. These were strange people, too. Fifty-six Vandyke Crescent didn't seem like home any more. It was becoming increasingly influenced by Mr Ashley Reeves and, with his woman here too, Peta was the intruder. She'd have to move away. All the things she had worked to preserve for the memory of her parents were just ebbing away under her nose.

'I can't get warm since coming back to England,' Aileen said. 'Tenerife is wonderful to go to in winter. Have you been abroad to work, Peta?'

Peta looked at the doctor for the first time. She was very beautiful and would have been even without the tan. Why wasn't she showing signs of contempt at Peta's presence? But she had a warm personality, Peta noticed.

'No,' Peta answered, 'not to work, or for a holiday.'

'Peta lived here with her parents,' Ashley explained, lounging in a chair close to the gas fire.

Why couldn't he let her speak for herself for heaven's sake? With a spurt of confidence she said, 'I planned to do all sorts of things after I qualified, but Dad died soon afterwards, and then Mum needed me at home. But now I'm free, so I'm thinking of revising some of my old plans.'

'Such as?' Ashley asked slowly and in a tone that hinted of disbelief.

'New Zealand very probably,' she said, thinking 'as far away from you as possible'!

But she knew that she didn't mean that. In fact, when she finally got away—and then only because Snudgie was outside demanding his supper—she buried her face in his lovely cuddly coat and cried. She didn't want to go away anywhere, she wanted to stay as close to Ashley as possible. In such a short time he had become a very important person to her. All this talk about not wanting him to concern himself over her was quite untrue. She liked being 'managed', she wanted him to look after her. And instead he was downstairs, probably at this minute making love to the sophisticated Aileen.

It became much warmer during the night. Peta woke to hear the rain and melting snow dripping off the roof and later a frightening thud as a great load swooshed to the ground. And then she remembered who was in the ground floor flat. She turned over and buried her face in the pillows to try to shut out her thoughts but they persisted, and she didn't manage to go to sleep again. It was easier to be up and about, though she tried not to make any noise. She had time to prepare vegetables and set the oven to come on mid-morning so that her lunch would be ready when she came home at noon.

There were no movements when she let herself out of the house quietly at about seven-thirty. She always backed the car into the garage just as her father had taught her to do, so now, with the engine running smoothly, she was able to drive out without any undue revving. It was nice to have the car on the road again and it helped to restore her confidence, and once on duty she went to see her favourite baby. She bathed and fed him herself while he gurgled happily and she was hardly finished when Nurse Kray came to tell her she was wanted on the telephone.

Peta put Marty back in his cot and hurried to her office.

'Sister Blair speaking,' she announced.

'Good morning, Pet, sorry to call you so early.'

There was no mistaking Quentin's voice.

'Nice to hear from you,' she said, 'but if you're looking for Ashley I'm afraid I haven't seen him yet this morning.'

'I'm not looking for my brother,' Quentin said positively, 'I'm ringing to ask you for a date. I have to travel up to Bath today so thought I'd come and see you for some home cooking on the way back.'

'I'm on split shift today,' she said.

'You're in charge—can't you alter that arrangement?'

'I don't like doing that,' she started hesitantly, but there was no reason why she shouldn't. Looking quickly at the duty rota pinned to the wall above her desk, she noticed that Cathy was on late turn. She couldn't pass up the chance of a date with Quentin, she decided. 'Um—well, I might just be able to wangle things,' she said. 'What time will you be arriving?'

'About six to six-thirty at a rough guess.'

With an upsurge of delight Peta agreed, and when Cathy came on duty just after midday Peta dashed home, had a cheese sandwich and rescued her chicken from the oven. She only had three-quarters of an hour but it was long enough to take out a second chicken portion from the fridge and prepare more fresh carrots to go with a packet of frozen green peas. On her way home at four-thirty she would have time to get some sprouts from the shop and then she would only need to prepare a lemon sorbet.

When she returned to the hospital she checked with the SNO that her change of duty was approved before going to the ward.

'Everything all right?' she asked her staff nurse. 'Sorry I'm a few minutes late but I thought I'd better notify the SNO of the change of duty.'

'Mrs Alexander telephoned,' Cathy said, looking puzzled. 'She seemed to think that Marty might be able to go home today. I told her that I hadn't heard anything about it, so she's going to ring again at two o'clock.'

'I haven't had confirmation from Mr Reeves. Hasn't he been round yet?'

'No.'

Peta glanced at her watch and bit on her lip. She hoped he'd appear before two. He didn't have a specific clinic today and it wasn't his theatre day. There had been no one at home she thought, so had he gone off with Aileen somewhere? Normally he put his duties at Gida's before all else, especially now that Christmas was over and the wards were almost full. Evidently Aileen had enough influence over him to take his mind off his work, and Peta didn't much care for those implications.

By two o'clock there was still no sign of him when Mrs Alexander telephoned again.

'I'm sorry,' Peta told her, 'I didn't know a definite date had been decided. Did Mr Reeves actually say *today*?'

'Well, yes,' Mrs Alexander faltered. 'The lady doctor who was with him suggested there was nothing to keep Marty in for now.'

'I'm really sorry, Mrs Alexander,' Peta said, 'but nothing definite was passed on to me, and unfortunately Mr Reeves hasn't been in today. He'll still be at lunch at present, but I'll see if I can track him down. You see, normally, we keep patients like

Marty here for two or three days after the stitches have been removed just to make sure the wound has completely healed. I think you had better come in as usual, but if I should find out anything different I'll phone you back before two-thirty.'

Peta had Ashley bleeped, not caring if he was at lunch, but every search proved negative. His houseman confirmed that he had not been in today and was not expected.

'So what made him give Mrs Alexander reason to think Marty could go home?' she asked Dave Gilbert testily.

'I wasn't there so how would I know?'

'When's he coming in?'

'He didn't say, but I'm sure Marty should stay for a further forty-eight hours.'

'Then you come and tell Mrs Alexander that.'

They argued for several minutes more. Such a misunderstanding was unusual but not unknown, and Peta felt convinced that Mrs Alexander had got hold of the wrong end of the stick, even though when she arrived she still insisted that Mr Reeves had agreed with the lady doctor, that, once the stitches were out Marty might as well be at home.

'I'm really sorry,' Peta apologised, 'but of course, Dr Palmer was only visiting. Marty isn't her patient so she may have voiced her thoughts, but it was in no way intended for you to take seriously. I promise you, Marty is doing very well indeed, but I don't have any powers to allow him home.'

Peta could see how disappointed the young mother was and she felt very angry with Ashley. Acting consultant or not, he'd have to be reminded of his responsibilities.

CHAPTER TEN

MR ASHLEY Reeves appeared to have gone missing! Peta's impatience grew to downright fury as, each time she had him bleeped, she received the same reply. No one knew where he was and no one but she cared! At the risk of making herself thoroughly unpopular she bullied houseman Dave Gilbert into having a chat with Mrs Alexander later that afternoon to reassure her that no deterioration in Marty's condition had occurred. Peta left at four-thirty, not entirely satisfied, but feeling she had done everything she could.

She drove home on dirty, slushy roads, carefully reversing up the drive and annoyed that Ashley's absence was obvious by the fact that his car wasn't in the garage. She wished she could have confronted him while she was still angry, and get it over with before Quentin arrived, but it wasn't to be. She got the dinner going, then had a shower and put on a beige wrap-around skirt and a burgundy coloured jumper which had silver embroidery edging the neck and shoulders.

The flat was comfortably warm without being overwhelmingly hot. At last she could forget about burst pipes and freezing temperatures, but now there was a new fear. Already in Cornwall and South Devon melting snow and rain coming in from the Atlantic was causing flooding. It was unlikely that their area, or even Gida's, would be affected, but Peta felt sorry for the people whose homes she saw awash on the television news while waiting for Quentin to arrive.

Everything was set for a cosy dinner with him, but Peta was confused in her thoughts. Quentin gave the impression that he was lively and exciting to be with, but she remembered she had been disappointed before. This time she intended to play it cool and expect nothing. And, of course, she didn't want anything from him, only enough to help her forget his brother. It wasn't going to be easy, but when Quentin arrived and was sitting opposite her enjoying the meal it became ever more difficult because there were mannerisms he and Ashley shared.

His lips, like his twin brother's, were smooth and sensuous and Quentin too had a lock of hair which fell forward just above one eye. Peta remembered thinking when she had first met Ashley that his hair had been allowed to grow too long in the back of his neck, but here at least Quentin's was different, for it was closely cropped.

'How's your day been?' Peta asked him.

'Oh, so-so. Ironing out difficulties on behalf of the unit. What about yours?'

Peta laughed. 'Sounds a little like yours. Ironing out problems created by your brother.' She went on to explain in detail.

Quentin listened attentively with a grim expression.

'Poor old Ashley. That doesn't sound like him. I mean, not letting his personal life interfere with his work.'

Peta toyed with the last few bites of succulent chicken.

'Women trouble?' she asked in a low voice without daring to meet Quentin's gaze.

'*Woman* trouble—possibly,' he said.

'Not Dr Palmer by any chance?'

'How did you know about Aileen?' Quentin asked in surprise. 'He usually keeps his love life very private.'

Peta cringed. Love life! So Aileen Palmer was the special love of his life. Peta tried not to sound too curious but she told Quentin about their visit to Gida's, carefully avoiding the fact that she had been pressed into joining them for a drink.

'Is—um—is Dr Palmer an old or new friend?' she asked hesitantly. 'Or more than a friend?'

Quentin sighed. 'I doubt that Ash would approve of me telling—'

'Then please don't,' Peta begged, cutting in, suddenly deciding that perhaps she'd rather not know.

'Perhaps I should as he's your tenant, and I suppose in a way your boss too.'

'Dr Mandeville is *that*, if anyone is, until I'm told differently.'

'But it's only fair that you should make allowances, Pet—for the time being.'

'Where human life is concerned there are no excuses,' she said emphatically. She was aware of Quentin staring directly at her.

'My, my, you have got it in for poor old Ash.'

'He isn't poor and he isn't old,' Peta snapped.

There was a pause, with tension mounting between them, until Quentin laughed.

'No, thirty-five isn't old.'

'And neither of you married.' She tut-tutted scornfully.

'*I'm* not the marrying kind.' Well, that was telling her flatly, she thought. At least now she knew that there need be no more pretence. 'But Ashley was nearly married, four years ago—to Aileen.'

Peta reproached herself for being inquisitive. She didn't need or want to know any more.

'So now they're going to pick up where they left off?' That was what she *did* need to know.

'Aileen's come here to build bridges.' He sighed. 'I'm ashamed to say it was all my fault.'

'Good heavens!' Peta exclaimed. 'You can't be blamed for your brother's mistakes just because you're a twin.'

'You don't listen,' he told her impatiently. 'I must tell you the truth or you'll get hold of the wrong end of the stick—though I'm sure you understand this isn't for public broadcasting.'

It wasn't often that Quentin was so serious. Now that he was he seemed more like Ashley.

'I'm a flirt,' he announced. 'I make no apology for that. I like women, but I live in a man's world, so the two things have to be kept separate—or that's my philosophy. Unfortunately, when Aileen and I embarked upon a few secret assignations she expected me to whisk her up the aisle, and she let it all out to Ash in the heat of an argument. I didn't want things to go that far. I certainly never considered marrying Aileen, and after that neither did Ashley.'

'Instead he went to Africa,' Peta said slowly, feeling emotionally overturned at such admissions from Quentin.

'Ashley intended to go anyway. Aileen was being encouraged to go with him, as a husband and wife team, but in a way that's how she and I became close, because she just had to confide in someone that she didn't want to go.'

'Surely—if they really loved one another they should have been honest with each other?' Peta suggested.

'That is how lovers should behave, Pet, but few of us have the courage to be totally honest. Anyway, when Aileen discovered that I had no intention of ever getting married, she got a job in a private clinic in Tenerife.'

'And your parents went there for Christmas?'

'To lure Ash there—yes,' Quentin agreed. 'Everyone trying to erect that bridge, you see, which I had broken down. Though I'm bound to say it would have disintegrated eventually.'

'How can you be so sure?'

'Because I know the two people concerned better than anyone else.'

'But now the bridge is being repaired?'

Quentin raised his eyebrows and gazed at her with an intensity which she found embarrassing. He sighed. 'It looks like it, and I'm sorry.'

'Why?' Peta felt the colour flushing her cheeks.

'Because I think it will be a mistake,' he answered slowly and deliberately, not wanting to embarrass her.

Peta had enjoyed her meal but she got up hurriedly, taking the used plates and dishes to the kitchen. As she put the coffee on and carried the glass dishes containing the lemon sorbet to the table, she felt a gnawing ache creeping upwards from somewhere deep inside her. It reached her throat and eyes, constricting her facial muscles. She wouldn't cry—of course she wouldn't. You didn't weep over losing something you'd never had—and yet she felt as if life had cheated her out of something very precious.

Love is our most cherished emotion, she silently conceded, finally confessing that the growing pain in her heart was love for Ashley. Damn him—she didn't want to love him. She had tried to steer aggression to hate but he had done everything to win her love, when all the time he was planning a come-back with Aileen.

'He might just as well have gone to Tenerife for Christmas,' she said, voicing her grudging thoughts.

'He's done everything to avoid seeing Aileen again. She came here to test him out because he wouldn't go to Tenerife,' Quentin divulged.

'And found his weak spot,' Peta muttered. Then, with a conciliatory note, 'She is extremely beautiful.'

'Aileen is a charming person,' Quentin said thoughtfully.

Peta looked quickly across at Quentin. That had come from the heart. Was it possible that here they were, two lost souls pining for two other people who were about to make a leap into the future? A leap straight into the slough of despond!

Was it possible that Quentin was more capable of loving than he cared to admit? Was all this philandering a cover-up to hide the hurt? Peta could only speculate. She knew neither of them well enough to know what they really felt. She only knew without doubt that she loved Ashley Reeves more than any man she had ever met. She would never be able to tell Ivor just how close he had come to arranging the perfect partner for her. She felt desolate, but this wasn't the way to entertain a friend, and a friend who needed livening up.

She cleared the table and they sat in easy chairs to enjoy their coffee. Soon they were laughing again; Quentin was good for her and she hoped that in some small way she might be helping him if he did genuinely love Aileen. But her pain still persisted, however cleverly she hid it from the world.

It was well past eleven when Quentin decided to leave. Peta had watched the clock for the past hour, but he appeared not to have noticed. Then she woke up to the fact that Ashley hadn't returned and Quentin might be waiting to see him.

'I haven't heard your brother come home,' she ventured to say as she followed Quentin down the stairs.

'He's taken Aileen to stay with my parents—he may not return until tomorrow.'

In the porch, under the light which Peta had switched on, Quentin held her fast as he smiled down at her.

·'Thanks for your company, Peta, and the meal. I'd love to see you again as long as you realise that I'm guilty of being frivolous, and there's nothing serious in our relationship.'

'I think it's a mutual feeling,' she said, placing her hands on his arms as he held her closer.

He was just a nice, interesting man, she thought as she felt his body meet peaceably with hers. He reached down from his lofty height and kissed her warmly but without any real passion. He whispered that he would be in touch and they went into a friendly clinch again, just as headlights arced round in the Crescent and Ashley's car splashed noisily into the drive.

'I'd better just say hello,' Quentin whispered, and followed Ashley up the driveway to the garage.

Peta remained half hidden in the porch, listening to the low murmur of the brothers' voices. The next minute Quentin strode out to his car.

'Night, Peta, see you,' he called, and Ashley watched him go from the outside gates which he closed. Peta wasn't quite speedy enough to get inside before Ashley reached his front door.

'I hope you know what you're doing?' he grunted. 'Don't say I haven't warned you—Quentin doesn't treat women seriously.'

'I've yet to meet the man who does,' she snapped back. 'And who I entertain is my affair. You seem to do what you like in the downstairs flat, *and* you treat people with little consideration.'

She hadn't intended to provoke him into a fight in the front porch. She, standing half in, half out of her flat, and Ashley in a similar position in his, but his arrogant attitude brought out all the hostility again.

'What's that supposed to mean?' he demanded.

'Mrs Alexander seemed to be expecting to take Marty home today.'

'I hope you didn't let her.'

'No, but it's no thanks to you. Fancy not having the decency to confer with me after Dr Palmer had apparently suggested that she considered he could be discharged!'

'You should know better than to accept the advice of a visitor—and stranger at that.'

'I didn't actually hear her say any such thing.'

'No—because you were rude enough to walk away.'

'She was your visitor,' Peta declared haughtily.

'She's my friend, and I did expect you to have the courtesy to be polite.'

'And I consider I was—and now you can see, Mr Reeves, exactly why I didn't want anyone connected with the hospital living here.'

'Yes, because *you* want to be in control.'

'It is my house,' she yelled, 'though not for much longer. If I go abroad to work it will have to be sold.' God! Now she'd just gone too far. She went inside, slamming the door and fumbling with the bolts and safety chain. At least she was making it clear that she meant him to keep out.

For a few minutes she stood with her back against the door. The large hall had been divided between the two flats by a solid brick wall so she couldn't hear what Ashley was doing. As if it mattered, she thought despondently. But it did—that was the crux of the matter. She felt guilty at having entertained Quentin here when Ashley so obviously disapproved. How would he ever know how much she loved him if she carried on and responded to Quentin's flirting?

She crept miserably up the stairs with a heavy heart. He wouldn't want to know. He had Aileen; but at least he hadn't done the pursuing. It seemed that he had done everything to avoid rebuilding the bridge Quentin had talked about, but now that Aileen had come running after him it was clear enough that the bridge was well established or he wouldn't have taken her to stay with his parents.

Peta felt totally defeated. Like Quentin she had been outmatched. Yet Quentin had obviously not made the most of his opportunities. If he really cared for Aileen as he had implied, he could have rebuilt that particular bridge over the past four years while Ashley was in Africa. Maybe he was sincere in his decision to remain a bachelor.

Peta tried to hide her emotions by putting up a brave front next day, but she knew that she was being unsociable with her colleagues and short-tempered with the nurses under her, which was unusual.

One of the new pupil nurses had made a mess of Paul Newton's charts and Peta was taking her to task severely over it, and as she turned to leave the small one-bedded room she collided with a hard, immovable object. Masculine arms imprisoned her, danced her round in a half-circle to avoid a painful clash.

'In any other circumstances, I'd say let's dance,' Ashley said. 'Good afternoon, Sister.' He remained supporting her. The blood rushed to her cheeks at the close contact. She could smell his cologne and her body reacted pleasurably to the nearness of his. Crazy thoughts rushed round in her brain. Her fingertips tingled with a desire to slide her fingers underneath his waistcoat. She wanted to feel him . . .

'Good afternoon,' she mumbled incoherently.

'Hello, Paul, sitting up and taking notice?' Ashley said as he went to look for the chart at the end of the bed.

'I'm afraid it needs re-doing . . .' Peta began.

Ashley looked from Peta to the equally scarlet

face of the young nurse. He raised one eyebrow and made a funny face at her.

'You in Sister's bad books too?' he whispered conspiratorially. 'Have to find a way of sweetening her up, won't we?' He patted the girl's shoulder. 'Never mind, Nurse, we all make mistakes, even our efficient Sister Blair.'

Peta's cheeks burned. He would never let her forget that she'd been wrong about Marty Alexander. To avoid any further aggravation Peta pushed the chart into Ashley's hand.

'I'm sure Nurse will be able to explain anything you may need to know,' she said, and walked away.

'Tea, please, Nurse Kray,' she called as she passed the kitchen, though she hoped Ashley's visit would be short.

A few minutes later he strolled nonchalently into her office and put Paul's chart down on her desk.

'If I may make a suggestion, Sister, the nurse in question will learn more quickly if you let her re-do the chart herself.'

Peta only glanced up casually from her work, now in complete control again.

'That's exactly what I intended,' she said disinterestedly. 'Tea is on the way.'

'Splendid, but first, if Mrs Alexander's here I'd like to see her.'

'She's here. Do you need me?'

When he didn't give an immediate response Peta glanced up. His deep, taunting eyes regarded her without a hint of meaning.

'Not if you're too busy. I thought you might like to see that I believe in honesty, and am not too proud to admit to my mistakes, though in this

particular instance I think Mrs Alexander miscon-
strued what Aileen said.' He started for the door,
then looked back. 'In your expert opinion is there
any reason why Marty shouldn't go home today?'

'None at all.'

'Sorry, darling, but he can't stay here for ever,'
he said softly.

She heard his light tread fade as he went into the
ward. He must have different shoes on today as she
hadn't even heard him approaching Angelique
ward. Her heart had fluttered and skipped a beat at
his term of endearment. It meant nothing, she
thought sadly, he probably had Aileen on his mind.

She was drinking her tea when he returned to the
office.

'Mrs Alexander tells me that Marty's in his own
clothes, so if you'll be kind enough to allow her to
use the telephone later she'll get her husband to
come and pick them up. I'm discharging him as of
now. I'll have that cup of tea, do a quick round with
you and then I'm off.'

He sat down in the chair close to her desk, and
with a none too steady hand she poured the tea.

'I thought you were much too involved with this
hospital now to want to leave it,' he added, stirring
his tea thoughtfully.

Peta busied herself with some paperwork. She
couldn't bear to look at him. Of course she was too
involved with Gida's to want to leave, but she
couldn't stay and have to watch him and Aileen
together.

'It doesn't do to get in a rut,' she replied abruptly.

'I understood you couldn't bear the thought of selling your home.'

'Circumstances change. I realise if I'm to widen my horizon I must do it soon.' She drained her cup hurriedly, endeavouring to give him the impression that she had a lot to do.

He drank his tea in silent concentration.

'Stephanie's being admitted at the weekend,' he said. 'With another child of about the same age. A few months older, but a more mature child, the eldest of three children. We'll have all the family in for tests eventually, of course, but I would like to see a friendship established between Stephanie and Amanda. I hoped we'd be a team—two people who they could rely on. Still, if you've made up your mind.'

Peta felt an awful restriction in her throat and couldn't trust herself to speak, but he was waiting for her reaction.

'I shan't be going yet,' she said in a croaky voice. 'I'm not in a position to just up and go.'

She poured out another half a cup of tea for herself to steady her nerves.

'Perhaps we could discuss your plans in more detail at home.'

Her stomach muscles tightened at the way he used the word 'home'.

'There's nothing to discuss,' she retorted crisply.

Ashley put his cup and saucer back on the tray and stood up.

'I have several things to say to you, but not while you're being so damnably trying. You need a holiday or a couple of days off, Peta. It's not like you to be so blasted obstinate. I've apologised to Mrs

Alexander for the misunderstanding and she was quite charming about it, so there's no need for you to be so stuffy. I suppose it's the after-effects of Christmas, the weather, or maybe you're missing Dr Mandeville. I'm sure he'd be most flattered. Now, I'm in a hurry, so can we get on?'

Peta pushed back her chair. Maybe he was right about one thing. She felt intolerably weary, and the thought of her weekend off duty approaching had a certain attraction about it.

Ashley stood back and allowed her to pass into the ward first, but while he was chatting to the children she had a chance to look at him with more than just a critical eye. He was loose-limbed, his fingers long with well-manicured nails, and his navy blue pin-striped suit did everything to accentuate the leanness of his body and the length of his legs. He had just the hint of an arrogant swagger—well, wasn't he the most arrogant man she had ever met? The most handsome, the most lovable—but *she* couldn't have him.

Peta wondered why he had suggested they work together as a team when he would soon have Aileen as his partner. He was trying to placate her over the business with Mrs Alexander, she supposed. And there was Marty's young mum, smiling at Ashley coyly. Oh, he knew how to charm the women all right, Peta thought savagely.

They moved to each bed or cot, Peta managing to give him the information he required about each young patient, and finally he left, saying as she escorted him to the double doors, 'What time are you off duty?'

'Nine o'clock.'

'And what's the latest news of Mrs Hubbard?'

'Doing very well, keeping everyone at the convalescent home up to the mark, and looking forward to coming home.'

'A remarkable lady. She'll miss you when you go abroad and sell up.'

He caught Peta off guard. She opened her mouth to question his statement, but fortunately he had reminded her in time. She knew by the glint of wickedness in his eyes that he didn't believe her any more than she believed it herself. Now, if he had asked her to go to Africa with him . . .

'We'll have that discussion, Peta, just as soon as we can arrange it,' he said.

'I'll probably be going to visit my brother for the weekend.' How easily and quickly she could create lies, she thought with reproach.

'Splendid, that will do you good,' he said and ran his hand over her back in an affectionate gesture before pushing open the swing doors.

If only he realised what he was doing to her! Making up stories, putting herself before her patients, causing her to hate Aileen Palmer when she was most likely a charming woman, as Quentin had intimated. Yes, a weekend right away from Gida's was exactly what she needed, but with Ivor, Ros and the children? The moment her spirits had lifted, such a proposition dashed them to an all time low.

CHAPTER ELEVEN

THE NEXT day was Ashley's theatre day so the ward was in a mild state of chaos, and on Friday Peta had to try to fit in her paper-work when she could, in between post-operative nursing and fretful children. She should have left at one o'clock, having a half day off before her weekend, but it was well after three when Cathy scolded her.

'Sister, you must go home,' she said. 'You look all in. Are you doing anything special this weekend?'

'I may go to Brighton. On the other hand I may leave it until the early spring and go for a week. I feel undecided.' May as well keep up the pretence. Peta thought. Across the bed they were making, Peta looked closer at Cathy.

'You look very pleased with yourself,' she said with a warm smile, reacting to the more junior girl's sparkle.

'I've got every reason to. I was going to tell you the other day, but you didn't seem yourself— you've been preoccupied. But, I'm sure you'll be pleased. Glenn and I are getting engaged on Sunday when I go home. I'm on early shift. We were going to ask you for drinks.'

'Who? Who's Glenn?'

'Oh, *Sister*! You know, the Marine corporal who came to put up the decorations at Christmas.'

'But, Cathy! That's quick work. Are you sure?'

Peta stopped, despising herself for her lack of enthusiasm. 'Oh, Cathy, I'm sorry. I'm thrilled for you both! *You*, of all people,' she said, and they laughed together.

'I meant to ask you, and I wondered whether Mr Reeves' brother would have liked to come too, only I don't know . . .' her voice trailed off and her cheeks became very pink.

Peta laughed again. 'What the situation is,' she filled in for Cathy. 'We're just good friends, Quentin and I,' she went on. 'We would have come if I hadn't been going away. Thanks for asking us. I'm sure you'll have a marvellous time.'

As she drove home, Peta felt angry with herself. She had been a misery these past few days. Cathy didn't deserve such treatment, she was a nice girl and a most competent nurse. She ought to have noticed the excitement reflected in her expression. She sighed as she put the car away. She had no intention of going to Brighton, but in her state of mind she didn't feel she could participate in anyone else's happiness.

She went into her flat, noticing that Ashley's car wasn't in the garage. He had probably gone wherever Aileen was for the weekend. It was going to be hellishly lonely—but didn't she have Snudgie? At least he didn't argue with her. He just gave her the love she needed. He cried plaintively now as he put his front paws round her arm and stretched up to the draining-board where she emptied the last of a tin of cat food on to his plate.

Peta made herself a cup of tea and carried it into her lounge, and when Snudgie had finished his meal he came to her for more.

'You're a greedy pig,' she told him, and when she bent down to stroke him he purred happily, put his two front paws gently round her face and rubbed his cheek against hers. He was a darling, but eventually he'd have to go back to Mrs Hubbard, just as Marty had gone home with his parents—and Ashley to his Aileen. Always the loser, she told herself with a touch of self-pity.

She put down some more food for the cat, but he ate only a small portion, then spent half an hour carrying out his ablutions meticulously before deciding that it was time to play.

As long as Ashley was out, Peta didn't mind romping with Snudgie, often on all fours, playing peek-a-boo behind the kitchen door. She'd made many a snide remark about people going soft with their pets, yet here she was, chatting to Snudgie as if he understood every word. He did, of course, she told him. He was a very intelligent cat for only fifteen months. A true tiger tabby with a mixture of long Persian hair which made him all the more cuddly. But for some reason she wouldn't have liked Ashley to see her playing with him or hear her talking to him.

It was getting dark when she let him out of the front door and then she went back upstairs. Although there were many jobs about the flat which she had promised herself she would do, she felt idle and couldn't find the energy to do anything except put her feet up and watch television.

It was unlike Peta, but she must have dropped off to sleep and woke with panic when the doorbell rang. It took her several minutes to collect herself enough to go downstairs. She had changed into stretch jeans and a warm sweater earlier, and now she padded down the stairs in her stockinged feet so that the caller didn't hear her coming and rang again with an extra long peal.

'I'm coming,' she called impatiently and opened the door to find Ashley in the porch, cradling Snudgie in his arms.

'Whatever's happened?' she asked, peering anxiously at the cat.

'Nothing,' Ashley said casually. 'He's been with me for half an hour or so since I came in. He was sitting hopefully in the porch so I've given him some supper—a few pieces of left-over bacon.'

'But I fed him when I came home,' she said. 'He just never stops eating.'

'And what about his adoptive mum—has she eaten?'

'Mm—yes,' she lied.

Ashley's voice held a familiar ring of joviality.

'You're the biggest liar I ever met,' he said. 'You haven't eaten, you look half-starved and half-asleep, and our little friend here is asking you to supper.'

Peta hesitated. 'I . . . I'm packing to go to Brighton,' she said quickly.

'Then it's all the more important that I discuss my plans with you before you go.'

He stood there waiting and she knew he would only go on worrying her until she agreed. She didn't have the courage to tell him that she knew he wanted to tell her about him and Aileen.

'I'll come down in a few minutes,' she said.

'I'll leave the door on the latch, come straight in.'

He retreated into his flat still nursing Snudgie.

Peta combed her ash-blonde hair and fluffed it up. She applied a smudging of pale blue eyeshadow to match her chunky Shetland wool sweater and chose a pink lipstick to give herself a little colour. She didn't think it was quite the thing to visit her tenant in slippers, so she put on some navy blue crepe-soled walking shoes and, taking a deep breath, went downstairs. She must be brave. Above all she mustn't let him see how she felt.

'I think Snudgie has taken us over,' she said by way of introduction as she closed his front door and Snudgie leapt excitedly to greet her. 'I wouldn't have thought you'd have liked cats.'

'I'm human,' Ashley said and waited for her to walk towards the lounge door. He was wearing rich chocolate brown slacks with an oatmeal coloured sweater over a pale shirt. The sight of him in such domestic surroundings made her feel weak and she knew she ought to have stayed in her own part of the house. She had attached her key to a ring on the pocket of her jeans and they jangled slightly as she followed him unhurriedly into his lounge.

Candles and deep pink camellias in a glass bowl adorned the dining-table, which was set for two.

'I . . . I'm sorry. I must be intruding, you're expecting . . .'

'You, darling, but before we eat let's get down to business.'

'If it's to do with the flat,' she said, her mind a waterfall of confused suppositions, 'you ought to see Mr Fitzgerald.'

'I have, and I have two contracts for you to read

and sign. This one is to take effect if you go abroad to work, but I believe now that you concocted that story, so this one may seem more relevant.'

He pushed a long sheet of paper into her hand. It looked legal enough, headed with the estate agent's name and address, and below, after the legal jargon of *I hereby* and so on, the typewritten insert stunned her. *Mr and Mrs Ashley Reeves*, she read, and immediately her weakness became real. Her eyes filled with tears which for days now she had fought back. He was married, or getting married, and he was trying to buy her half of fifty-six Vandyke Crescent!

Peta couldn't bear it, she threw the paper against his chest impetuously.

'There are plenty of other houses you can buy if you're getting married,' she shouted at him, and with tears flowing fast she opened his front door and struggled to get her key off the ring at her hip, but she was blinded.

'Peta, darling—I'm sorry. The last thing I wanted to do is to upset you.' He caught her and pulled her back inside.

'Let me go, I want to go home,' she protested, fighting against him.

He held her face between his hands and forced her to look at him.

'You are home.' He shook his head impatiently. 'This is *our* home. I want it to be ours jointly when we get married.'

'We?' she whimpered stupidly. 'But Aileen?'

'Aileen, my dear, has returned to Tenerife.' He sighed and drew her back to the lounge, keeping her encircled in his arms. 'For four long years I've carried a candle for her, a bitter, twisted one, despising her and Quentin for their cheap little affair. I've only discovered now that she turned to him because she didn't want to go to Africa. I've also only just discovered that I never really cared for her in the way that I should have done, or *I* wouldn't have gone to Africa. What I have discovered, my sweet darling, is that I love you more than I have ever loved anyone—enough to go where ever *you* want to go.'

Peta sniffed. She didn't really believe a word he was saying.

'I . . . I don't want to go anywhere,' she said. 'I mean—oh, Ashley, I love you enough to follow you to the North Pole if necessary.'

She turned and clung to him in desperation. She didn't care if he didn't mean what he'd said, she couldn't hold back the truth any longer.

'But, darling, we don't need to go anywhere,' he said softly. 'I suppose Gida's and Angelique ward can stand the strain of a husband and wife working team—that is, until we have a baby of our own.'

He tilted her face up so that he could kiss her, gently at first. He was so tender that her body sang with expectation. She reached up and linked her arms lovingly around his neck.

Then he held her hands in his and whispered, 'Later, Pet. The candles are burning down. Let's eat.'

'The camellias don't look real,' she said. 'They look like ever-lasting flowers—and you pinched them from my garden,' she added, prodding him playfully.

'If you sign that contract,' he said, 'it's *our* garden, and our love will be as everlasting as eternity.' And they made love with passion-filled eyes through the flickering candle flame.

Mills & Boon

4 Doctor Nurse Romances
FREE

Coping with the daily tragedies and ordeals of a busy hospital, and sharing the satisfaction of a difficult job well done, people find themselves unexpectedly drawn together. Mills & Boon Doctor Nurse Romances capture perfectly the excitement, the intrigue and the emotions of modern medicine, that so often lead to overwhelming and blissful love. By becoming a regular reader of Mills & Boon Doctor Nurse Romances you can enjoy EIGHT superb new titles every two months plus a whole range of special benefits: your very own personal membership card, a free newsletter packed with recipes, competitions, bargain book offers, plus big cash savings.

AND an Introductory FREE GIFT for YOU.
Turn over the page for details.

**Fill in and send this coupon back today
and we'll send you**

4 Introductory
Doctor Nurse Romances yours to keep

FREE

At the same time we will reserve a
subscription to Mills & Boon
Doctor Nurse Romances for you. Every
two months you will receive the latest
8 new titles, delivered direct to your door.
You don't pay extra for delivery. Postage and
packing is always completely Free.
There is no obligation or commitment –
you receive books only for
as long as you want to.

**It's easy! Fill in the coupon below and return it to
MILLS & BOON READER SERVICE, FREEPOST, P.O. BOX 236,
CROYDON, SURREY CR9 9EL.**

**Please note: READERS IN SOUTH AFRICA write to
Mills & Boon Ltd., Postbag X3010,
Randburg 2125, S. Africa.**

FREE BOOKS CERTIFICATE

**To: Mills & Boon Reader Service, FREEPOST, P.O. Box 236,
Croydon, Surrey CR9 9EL.**

Please send me, free and without obligation, four Dr Nurse Romances, and reserve a
Reader Service Subscription for me. If I decide to subscribe I shall receive, following my free
parcel of books, eight new Dr Nurse Romances every two months for £8.00, post and
packing free. If I decide not to subscribe, I shall write to you within 10 days. The free books
are mine to keep in any case. I understand that I may cancel my subscription at any time
simply by writing to you. I am over 18 years of age.
Please write in BLOCK CAPITALS.

Name _____

Address _____

_____

_____ Postcode _____

SEND NO MONEY — TAKE NO RISKS

*Remember postcodes speed delivery. Offer applies in UK only and is not valid to
present subscribers. Mills & Boon reserve the right to exercise discretion
in granting membership. If price changes are necessary you will be noti-
fied. Offer expires 31st December 1984.*

8DN

EP1